# The Road to Home

*Also by*
*Mary Jane Auch*

JOURNEY TO NOWHERE
FROZEN SUMMER

# The
# Road to Home

*Mary Jane Auch*

HENRY HOLT AND COMPANY

7811

NEW YORK

*I owe special thanks to the following people for their help in researching this book:*

*Cheryl Harness, author and illustrator of* The Amazing Impossible Erie Canal, *for lending me a whole carton of her Erie Canal notes and reference books;*

*Frank E. Przybycien, PE, author of* Utica: A City Worth Saving, *for information about the early buildings in Utica, New York;*

*fellow children's author Ellen Yeomans for helping sift through reference materials at the Rome Historical Society.*

Henry Holt and Company, LLC
*Publishers since 1866*
115 West 18th Street, New York, New York 10011

Henry Holt is a registered trademark of Henry Holt and Company, LLC
Copyright © 2000 by Mary Jane Auch. All rights reserved.
Published in Canada by Fitzhenry & Whiteside Ltd.,
195 Allstate Parkway, Markham, Ontario L3R 4T8

Library of Congress Cataloging-in-Publication Data
Auch, Mary Jane. The road to home / Mary Jane Auch.
p. cm.
Concluding book in the trilogy that comprises:
*Journey to nowhere* and *Frozen summer.*
Summary: In 1817, after her mother had died and her father abandoned his children,
thirteen-year-old Mem searches for a new home for Joshua, herself, and their
little sister. [Brothers and sisters—Fiction. 2. Fathers—Fiction. 3. Frontier and
pioneer life—New York (State)—Fiction. 4. New York (State)—Fiction.]
I. Title. PZ7.A898 Ro 2000 [Fic]—dc21 99-49230

ISBN 0-8050-4921-5 / First Edition—2000
Printed in the United States of America on acid-free paper. ∞
1 3 5 7 9 10 8 6 4 2

*To Phil Sadler, Ophelia Gilbert, and
all the friends I've made over the years at the
Warrensburg Children's Literature Festival*

# The Road to Home

# One

"Mem!" Papa called. "If we don't get on the road, we won't even make Canandaigua by nightfall."

I looked around our homestead—a rough log cabin in a clearing carved out of the forest. When Mama died last summer, Papa promised me we could go back home to our family in Connecticut. Since that day I had thought of nothing but getting away from this place that had brought us so much heartache. But now that we were leaving, my feet felt rooted to the ground. "Let me check the cabin one more time, Papa. I want to make sure we haven't forgotten anything."

It seemed strange for me to be responsible for doing the checking. When we left Connecticut the spring before last, Mama had been the one to count and recount every item to be packed, as Papa was too filled with the excitement of our wilderness adventure to pay attention to details. I had been only eleven then and not very helpful to Mama. But now it fell to me to make sure everything was loaded and ready to go.

I climbed the ladder to the loft that had been my sleeping place. I knew I wouldn't find anything. The only furniture had been my bed and dresser, and Papa had put them on the wagon this morning while I swept the last traces of us from the floors. The family who had bought our land would arrive tomorrow. I hoped this place would bring them more happiness than it had us.

"Hurry, Mem! Papa wants to leave." My younger brother, Joshua, had climbed the ladder.

"You're supposed to be watching Lily," I said.

I looked over his shoulder and saw Lily sitting on the dirt floor below. It was a little over a year ago that I had watched Lily's birth from this very spot. I hadn't known at the time that I would be more of a mother to her than Mama.

"Mem," Joshua insisted. "We're all ready except for you. Papa says we can get peppermint sticks at the store in Canandaigua if we get there before it closes."

"I wondered what had you so all-fired anxious to get going." Joshua was usually the one who dallied when we were trying to go somewhere. I followed him down the ladder, picked up Lily, and took one last look inside the cabin before I pulled the door shut.

Joshua had already climbed onto the wagon seat when I got there. I had started to hand Lily up to him when I felt something stop me. "Couldn't we go to Mama's grave before we leave, Papa?"

Papa put his arm around me. "We said our good-byes last night, Mem. You know your mama's in heaven, not buried back in that grave. You'll see more of your mama in your grandma's eyes than you will in a mound of dirt with her name on a marker."

"I know you're right," I said, "but it still pains me to leave her here like this." Mama was never meant for living in the wilderness. She missed her home and family so much, it drove her to madness. She grew distant and weak, unable to care for Lily or even herself. Finally she wandered off on a cold night and died from exposure. Even now, after almost a year without her, it was hard to believe we'd never see Mama again. Now we were going back to the place and people that Mama had loved. My heart ached that Mama couldn't go back with us. I lifted Lily up to Joshua and took my place walking beside Papa.

We were off again, heading toward Williamson, the walk I had taken every morning to go to school. After Mama couldn't be left alone, I had stopped going to school, but the teacher, Miss Becher, had boarded with us until Mama died. Then I had to stay home to care for Lily, but Miss Becher still came to our house at least once a week to help me with my studies. I wanted to stop at the school to thank Miss Becher for her help, but I knew Papa wouldn't want to wait while I talked to her. I'd have to get there before the wagon.

"Papa, may I run ahead to say good-bye to Miss Becher?"

"You'll have to be quick about it, Mem. We don't have time to stop and wait for you."

"You won't have to wait. I'll hurry." It wasn't hard to outdistance the team of oxen. With the heavy load in the wagon, they moved at a lumbering pace. I ran all the way into town and stopped just for a moment to catch my breath and smooth my hair before going to the school.

Miss Becher looked up as I opened the door. "Mem! I was hoping you'd stop by. Boys and girls, some of you may know Remembrance Nye. Her family is moving back to Connecticut today."

The faces that turned to look at me stared blankly. Most of the students I knew had moved farther west after the freezing weather we had all last summer.

Miss Becher picked up something from her desk and came toward me. "Work on your lessons, boys and girls. I'll be right back." She led me outside and handed me a slim volume bound in soft leather the color of cream. "I want you to take this journal with you, Mem. It's a place for you to write down your thoughts. I've also copied some of my favorite poems into it."

"It's beautiful," I whispered. "I should be giving you a gift to thank you for all the things you've taught me."

Miss Becher smiled. "Just seeing how eagerly you learn has been gift enough for me. I hope you won't give up your dream of becoming a teacher."

"I won't, Miss Becher. Now that we'll be living with our family, I'll be free to go to school full-time while my aunts and Grandma help take care of Lily."

We were interrupted by the rattle of wagon wheels as Papa led the team into the center of town. "I have to go," I said.

Miss Becher hugged me. "Have a safe journey, Mem. Write to me when you get settled."

"I will." I turned and ran toward the wagon so she wouldn't see my tears.

"What's that in your hand?" Papa asked when I fell into step beside him.

"Miss Becher gave me a book." I clutched it tight to my chest. Papa's hands were stained from oiling the wagon wheels this morning, and I hoped he wouldn't want to hold it.

"Mmm," he said, squinting down the road. He didn't seem interested in my answer.

I looked back as we left Williamson. Only Miss Becher stood in the hot morning sun, waving to us. Nobody else took notice of our leaving. The town would go on as if we had never been a part of it, but I knew I was forever changed by what had happened to us here.

Joshua and I switched places so I could tend to Lily in the wagon. Now that she had learned to walk, she took much more of my attention, and she was vexed that she couldn't walk along the road beside Joshua. I tried to keep her entertained with a little rag doll I had made, but she only screamed and tried to pull herself up on the side of the wagon. "Shasha!" she wailed, that being the closest she could come to our brother's name. Joshua looked over his shoulder and grinned at her but kept going along with Papa.

"If you're not careful, you'll fall clean out of here the way I did on our last journey," I said. "Then you'll have to find your way alone." Lily stopped crying and looked at me, blinking, as if she were considering what I had just said. Then she tried to pull herself up on her chubby little legs again, screeching when I pried her fingers loose from the wagon boards. "Me walk!" she said over and over, with baby babble in between. Finally she tired of the struggle and curled up on the quilt, sucking her thumb, trying to glare at me even though her eyelids were getting heavy. For a baby who had looked like an angel when she was born, Lily was becoming quite a handful.

When she finally drifted off to sleep, I had a chance to lean back in the wagon and study the scenery as we moved along. I thought I would recognize landmarks from our first journey, but everything looked so different coming from this direction. I felt as if I were unwinding myself from a dream and wished that I could unravel all the things that had happened to us since we left Connecticut.

I could hardly let myself believe that we were really going home. I longed to see Grandma, Aunt Sally, Aunt Lydia, and our uncles and cousins. Mama looked like both of her sisters, especially Aunt Lydia. Seeing them would almost be like having Mama back again.

I only wished we could have started back sooner, right after the funeral, the way Papa had promised. We'd had so many fits and starts of moving. Papa had found a family to buy our land last September, but then he learned he could burn the trees he'd cut down and sell the ash for potash. I reminded Papa that we needed to get Lily home where I'd have help caring for her.

"We'll only stay a little bit longer," Papa had answered. "I've already gone to the trouble of cutting the trees. Why let another man profit from my hard work by selling the ashes? I'll just take the rest of this week to burn off our follow and collect the cash. That way I'll not be going back to your mother's relatives with empty pockets."

I knew Papa hated to admit he had failed on our farm, so I stopped making a fuss about leaving. But when Papa saw how much money he could get for ashes, he decided to cut and burn more trees. Then the buyer got tired of waiting and went off to find another piece of land.

"That's for the best," Papa had said. "The more land I clear, the more the property will be worth when I sell it."

Days turned into weeks, and weeks into months. Soon we were caught in the dead of winter, with no buyers in sight. It was bitter cold and so terribly lonely. Only Miss Becher's visits made the time bearable. Then spring came, a real spring, not like last year with snows and killing frost. Before I knew it, Papa had plowed up the land where he had cut the trees. Soon he was talking of planting, and I feared he was fixing to stay forever.

It was Miss Becher who saved us. When she heard that her cousin was planning to move to the Genesee Country from Massachusetts, she put him in touch with Papa. After sending letters back and forth for weeks, Papa sold the farm to him. We had a mad flurry of packing, and here we were, heading home at last.

The bumping of the wheels on the corduroy road to Canandaigua brought me out of my thoughts. Lily seemed to like the jouncing and snuggled down into the quilts, still fast asleep. It wasn't long before we could see the city of Canandaigua in the distance.

"We'll be stopping here for the night," Papa called back to me.

"Can we stay at the inn, Papa?" I asked. "I mean since we have the money and all."

"I'll not be spending my money on foolishness," Papa said. "Especially with the weather so fine. There may be stormy nights later when we'll need the shelter. We'll camp on the other side of town, by the lake." We drove down the main street, with fine houses on either side. Then we came to the shops.

Joshua had been dawdling, but now he ran to catch up to Papa and tugged on his sleeve. "There's the store where we get candy, Papa."

"I just said we're not wasting money on foolishness."

"But Papa," Joshua persisted. "Couldn't we get a treat for Lily?"

"And what sort of treat did you have in mind?"

"I could help her eat one of those peppermint sticks."

"Ah, she'd need help with it, you think?"

"Well, she's too little to hold it by herself. I could make sure she didn't drop it."

Papa smiled. I could tell Joshua had softened his resolve. Sure enough, he pulled up the team in front of the general store, and I woke Lily to take her inside. Her eyes grew wide when she saw the shelves of goods, but that was nothing compared to the way she looked when she tasted the candy. She made a face at first, then grabbed the stick with both hands. We couldn't get her to let go of it until she went to sleep that night. By that time she was fairly covered with sticky peppermint.

After that, Papa stood by his decision to save money. I cooked all of our meals over a fire. We camped out the next night in Camillus. Papa had hoped to get as far as Rome by Thursday night, but we ran out of daylight and settled for a campsite in a grove of beech trees.

I had a hard time getting to sleep because of the mosquitoes buzzing around our ears. Then, just as the first light of dawn glowed in the east, the boom of a nearby cannon jolted us awake.

"Papa!" I screamed. "What's happening?"

Papa pulled on his britches and boots and loaded his shotgun. "You stay here with the young ones, Mem. I'll see what's going on."

I grabbed his wrist. "Don't go, Papa. You might be shot."

"Nothing will happen to me. Just stay in the wagon, hear? Don't move a step away from here until I come back and tell you it's safe."

"All right, Papa."

Lily was just starting to stir, and I saw that Joshua was trying to hold back tears. I put my arms around both of them, and we huddled together, watching Papa stride into the distance as the cannon boomed again.

"Is Papa going to die?" Joshua asked, his voice catching in his throat.

"No, Joshua. He'll see what's going on and come back to us, that's all. It won't take long." I smiled, trying to hide the fact that I didn't believe a word I had just uttered. The cannon boomed again. I held my breath, waiting to hear Papa's returning shot, but there was only silence. We had already lost our mama. Now had we lost Papa, too?

# Two

"Listen," Joshua whispered. "I hear music. Do they have music in battles?"

There was another cannon volley, and this time Papa appeared, running toward us through the grove of trees.

Joshua's fingers tightened on my arm. "They're chasing Papa!"

Papa was shouting something and motioning to us, but I couldn't make out what he was saying until he was almost to the wagon. "Dress quickly, children. You must come see this."

"Is it a war, Papa?" Joshua asked.

Papa stowed the gun in the wagon and called something over his shoulder as he ran off again, but I couldn't understand what he said. I quickly slipped on my dress and fastened the drawstring, then picked up Lily. Joshua was already following Papa through the grove of trees.

When we came out on the other side, we saw a crowd of people standing in the middle of a meadow, surrounded by yellow buttercups and purple clover. Surely this was no battle, for there were both men and women. They were all dressed in finery, the men in tall silk hats. One of the men was giving a speech as we drew closer. "By this great highway unborn millions will easily transport their surplus productions to the shores of the Atlantic. . . ."

"What's he talking about, Papa?" I whispered. "There's no highway here."

"He's talking about the Great Canal, Mem. They're starting to dig it right now. Right on this very spot."

The man giving the speech drove his spade into the ground, and soon all of the men were grabbing shovels and spades and vying with each other to see who could dig up the most clods. The cannon boomed again, and a coronet band struck up a march.

I had heard about the Great Canal in school. DeWitt Clinton had traveled across the state before he became governor, helping to survey a route. He said it would make New York the greatest state in the nation. I couldn't see how this little trench in the middle of a flat meadow could grow into something so important.

Papa talked with the man who had given the speech, then came back to us, his face flushed with excitement. "I just talked to Judge John Richardson. He's been awarded the first contract to build a section of the canal.

He's hiring men right now. He's paying thirty-seven-and-a-half cents a day, but he said if I'm an extra-good worker, I could make as much as half a dollar."

Lily squirmed in my arms until I let her down in a patch of clover. "But, Papa, we have to get home. The whole family is expecting us to be there within a fortnight."

"I'll send them a post telling them we've been delayed. We won't stay long. I can't pass up this opportunity, Mem. I've been hearing about this canal since before the war. That's why I wanted to come by Rome on the way back."

"You knew about this all along?" I asked.

"I knew they'd start digging soon. I didn't know I'd have the good fortune to get work, though. The more money I can make here, the sooner I'll be able to buy us our own farm in Connecticut. Farms go for a higher price there than I was able to get for our homestead. Even a few days' work will give me some extra money in my pocket." The early morning sun made Papa's eyes sparkle. It was the same look I'd seen on his face when he told us about the wonders of the Genesee Country two years ago. I was afraid that Papa had a new dream.

∞    ∞    ∞

After the ceremonies were over, we drove on into the city of Rome. We passed over a bridge and came to an intersection with a three-story wooden frame building. The sign said American Hotel. There was a well dug right in the dirt road with a curb around it and a wooden watering trough for animals. This corner seemed to be a center of activity, with a number of people going in and out of the hotel.

"Can we stay there, Papa?" Joshua asked. "It looks like a fine place."

"With fine prices to match," Papa said. "We don't need anything so grand. I'm sure we'll find a small tavern that's to our liking."

Several dozen houses and shops were lined up along both sides of Dominick Street, which appeared to be the main thoroughfare. Papa pulled up the wagon in front of a shabby two-story frame house with a sign over the door that said Tucker's Tavern. Joshua pouted but knew better than to complain.

"You mind the children, Mem. I'll see if we can get a room here," Papa said. A few minutes later he stuck his head out of the door and motioned for us to come in. I gathered up Lily and Joshua, and we climbed the stoop and went inside. There was a dingy parlor to the right and a large dining room with tables to the left. Beyond the dining room I could see a big kitchen in the back. Papa was standing in the dining room with a woman. "These are my children, ma'am," he said to her. "Mem is the oldest, then Joshua and the babe, Lily. Mrs. Maude Tucker owns this tavern, children, and she says she has a room for us."

Maude Tucker stood with her hands on her hips, giving us a good looking over. I looked her over, too. She was a large woman, not fleshy but big boned, with hands like a man's, the fingernails all split and broken. She had a wild mop of red hair that was carelessly pinned into a bun of sorts on top of her head and gray eyes that seemed to look right through a person. I knew right away that I didn't like her.

"Follow me, and I'll show you the only room I have left," Maude said. "If you'd come in yesterday, you could've had a bigger one." She led us upstairs to a pigeonhole of a space that was barely large enough to hold one lumpy bed with a dirty quilt, a bedside table, and a cot. The eaves cut down so sharply that Papa could only stand up straight by the wall with the door. The midday sun pushed hot air through the only small window. Mama would have taken one look inside this place, packed us all back in the wagon, and made Papa drive on to the next tavern even if it was miles away and we were tired enough to sleep on a bed of pitchforks.

"It's powerful hot in here," Joshua said.

Maude leaned against the doorjamb and turned her attention from Joshua to Papa. "I can give a better price to people stayin' here than those just passin' through. I usually get twelve cents for the main meal of the day and six cents a day for a room. I charge another eighteen cents for stabling and feeding a team for the week."

"I'll make other arrangements for my wagon and team," Papa said.

Maude nodded. "Just you and the children, then. Course the children won't be eatin' as much as a man, so I'll figure it for two adults. I'll throw in breakfast and lunch for ten cents a day. And since the room is small, I'll give you that for four cents. Let's see. That would make the week's room and board . . ." She squinted one eye shut and bit her lip while she ciphered in her head. "That's twenty-six cents a day per person. Times two is fifty-two cents a day."

Papa's face didn't change, but I remembered him saying he'd be making thirty-seven-and-a-half cents a day on the canal. At this rate he'd be losing money. What would he do now, give up this foolishness of working on the canal or take us to an even shabbier place?

"That's still a high price for such crowded accommodations," Papa said. "Thank you for your time, Mrs. Tucker. We'll be moving on."

"Suit yourself, Mr. Nye. It's nothin' to me one way or t'other, but you'll be hard-pressed to find a room in Rome. Men are comin' into town every day, lookin' to work on the canal."

Just then Lily started fussing again. Maude held out her arms, and Lily went to her eagerly, calming down the second Maude held her. I'd have to teach Lily to be more wary of strangers.

"Well, aren't you the sweet little thing? I don't get to see many babies in here." Maude cooed at Lily for a minute, then looked up. "Mr. Nye, you seem like nice folks—not like the usual lot what's comin' in to work on the canal. Maybe I could give you a better price if the older girl gave me some help in the kitchen with the dishes and such."

I couldn't believe the nerve of this woman, thinking I'd be willing to work in her kitchen. And I didn't like her holding my sister, either. I tried to take Lily from her, but Lily turned and snuggled into Maude's shoulder.

"I suppose . . . ," Maude continued, rubbing her cheek against Lily's hair, "counting the girl's work toward the board, I could see my way clear to charge you just for one adult. Does twenty-six cents a day sound agreeable to you? Payable at the beginning of each week?"

I waited for Papa to turn down the offer, but instead he said something that made my heart sink. "Those arrangements will be fine, Mrs. Tucker."

"But Papa," I gasped. "I have to watch Lily and keep track of Joshua. I can't be doing kitchen work."

"You could work at night, after you get the young'uns to bed," Maude said. "That's when I need the most help."

Papa nodded. "That sounds reasonable."

Reasonable? It didn't sound reasonable to me. The only chance I had to be by myself was when Lily slept. Now I'd be spending that time doing kitchen chores? I'd always hated washing dishes under the best of conditions. I'd have to talk to Papa alone about it. Surely he'd see how unfair this was.

"Just one other thing," Maude said. "I ain't never let a room to a family where the children were left alone during the day, Mr. Nye. The other canal workers are here without their families." She fixed her sharp gaze on me. "You'll have to keep the little ones in your room or outside. I can't have them running underfoot in the dining room or kitchen. You eat your meals, then stay out the way, hear?"

"Yes, ma'am." I couldn't force myself to smile at her, but I managed to choke down all the things I wanted to say. There was no sense in getting into trouble by speaking my mind to this woman. If I did, no telling what kind of unpleasant chores she'd find for me in the kitchen. I could stand anything for a few days. Then we'd be off again, heading for home.

❧   ❧   ❧

What Maude lacked in housekeeping skills, she made up for as a cook. The supper that night was a delicious venison stew with crusty rye bread still warm from the oven. The dining room was crowded and noisy. When Maude came to our table, I noticed that she had left the drawstring on her dress loose so that her ample bosom almost spilled over as she leaned forward to serve the stew. I suspected that was the reason most of the boarders and patrons of the tavern were men. Now I was sure that Mama wouldn't have approved of this place. Maude Tucker definitely was not a proper lady.

As I watched the serving girl take load after load of dirty dishes to the kitchen, I knew I'd have to speak my piece to Papa. I got my chance when Papa took us for a walk around Rome after supper. As soon as we were away from the tavern and Joshua was running ahead out of earshot I made my plea. "Papa, please don't make me work for Maude Tucker."

"We have no choice, Mem. You heard what she was charging for the room and board. Even if I worked up to earning fifty cents a day, I'd be giving every penny I made to her and then some."

"Then maybe it isn't sensible for you to work on the canal. As long as it costs so much to stay here and all."

Papa stopped in his tracks. "I'll be the one decidin' what's sensible and what's not in this family. Is that understood?"

"Yes, Papa." The money mattered more than me. That I understood.

Papa didn't have to start work until Monday, so we had the next two days to explore Rome and the sur-rounding countryside. Maude said that my kitchen duties would begin Monday night, so I was free until then. It was the first time I remembered Papa having so much time to spend with us. Though I was vexed with him, he seemed happier than I'd seen him since Mama died.

Monday morning we had a good early breakfast, then Papa left for the canal site on a wagon with a dozen or so other workers. We went back to the room for a while, but it was already heating up and so cramped, Joshua did nothing but complain. "Couldn't I go out on my own, Mem? I won't get lost."

"All right, but stay right by the tavern. I'll let Lily take a nap and come outside later."

I tried stretching out on the bed with Lily, but she was in no mood to sleep. She kept pulling herself up to her feet until I finally gave up and took her downstairs. The day had already turned hot, and going out into the sun made Lily more irritable. I thought a cool cup of water might calm her, so I took her back inside. Lily's crying brought Maude from the kitchen the minute I stepped through the door. When Lily saw Maude with her flaming hair, she stopped crying at once and stared wide-eyed.

"Did you forget about keepin' the children outside?" Maude said, wiping her hands on her apron.

"My sister is thirsty. It's hot out there."

"There's a pump and a tin cup out back. You don't need to be trailing in here every time you need a swallow of water."

Two men came through the tavern entrance and greeted Maude, one putting his arm around her. "Ah, Maude, my beauty. I've waited all day to see you."

Maude a beauty? Was this man blind? Maude wasn't ugly, but it would be a far stretch of the imagination even to call her pretty. I watched as Maude grasped the man's wrist, slipped his arm over her head, and escaped his embrace. "All day, Silas? It's only nine o'clock in the morning."

"Ah but it seems like an eternity, my dear. Surely it must be almost time for the sun to set."

The man caught her around the waist this time, but Maude deftly slipped free. "Now, Silas, that's no way to treat a lady."

From what I had seen of Maude, she was anything but a lady. Still, it was interesting to watch her sidestep this man's approaches. I'd never had the opportunity to view such goings-on before. I took mental notes, thinking they might prove valuable if I ever found myself needing to fend off unwanted advances. This was information that Mama never would have taught me, but useful nonetheless.

Maude made her final escape by slipping behind the bar, closing the fold-down door between herself and Silas. Then she poured him a glass of whiskey, handing it to him with a smile. "I'm going to miss your tomfoolery, Silas."

The man took a big gulp but almost choked at her words. "Miss me? You're not barring me from coming in here the way they did at The Rome Coffee House, are you? You know I'm only jesting with you."

Maude laughed. "You're not the one leaving. I am. At least I hope I am. Been wanting to sell this place for a long time, and now I think I have my chance."

Maude leaving? I couldn't believe our luck. Maude and the man were speaking more softly now, and I tried to sneak closer to hear their conversation. I was becoming quite skilled at eavesdropping without being noticed. I often listened to travelers discussing the routes they had taken from New England and dreamed of the day we would follow those same turnpikes to our home.

As I moved into the dining room, Lily started to cry again. Maude looked up, frowned, and left the bar to come toward us. Then Lily leaned away from my grasp and reached for a vase of flowers on a side table. Maude lunged and caught it just before it tipped over. The sudden movement frightened Lily, and her wails filled the room.

"I know you have your hands full with that one," Maude said, "but she can't be in here disturbing my customers. Most of 'em come to this tavern for a little peace and quiet. That's what I aim to give 'em."

I jiggled Lily to calm her, but she only squalled louder.

"Take your sister outside and find something to do with her," Maude said. "Don't you have a little doll to keep her occupied?"

"No," I said. That was a lie, because Lily did have the crude little doll I had made of rags, but I didn't want her parading it around in front of people, exposing my lack of sewing skills.

Maude studied Lily for a moment, then pulled a blossom from a stalk of flowers in the vase. "Well, then we'll just have to make do with something else. Did you ever play with snapdragons?" Maude squeezed the side of the blossom, and the petals opened up like a mouth. "See? It's a little dragon." She opened and closed the mouth rapidly, making a high barking sound. "Yip-yip-yip-yip! Dragon's gonna git your nose!" she said, holding it out to Lily.

Lily squealed with delight, reaching for the flower.

"I didn't know dragons barked," I said, annoyed at Lily for finding the foolish trick amusing.

"Dragons can do anything you want them to." Maude raised her eyebrows. "Don't you know how to pretend? Come outside. I'll show you something else." She called into the kitchen for the serving girl to tend the bar, then motioned for me to follow her.

Pretending indeed. I hadn't had time for such foolishness since Lily's birth. I reluctantly trailed Maude out the door and around to the back of the tavern. Maude pointed to a thick row of tall, spiky flowers that ran across the back wall. "These here are hollyhocks."

I shifted Lily to my other hip. "I know." Who didn't know what hollyhocks were? Grandma had them all the way down her driveway, for heaven's sake.

Maude plucked a deep red blossom from the stalk. "You can make fine ladies from these," she said. "This is the skirt, then you need a spent blossom for the head." She searched the stalks until she found a wilted blossom all shriveled up to a long point. "You push it onto the stem like this, then twist the hair to fashion it." She held the finished doll in her hand. "See? If you look just the right way, it could be a lady in one of them ball gowns with her hair piled all high and fancy on her head."

Maude set the doll in the puddle under the pump and gave it a gentle push. "I like them in water best. See how she floats along so graceful like? You could make a whole parade of ladies. Pretend they're dancin' that newfangled waltz thing I've been hearin' so much about. You can use as many flowers as you want. Nobody sees 'em back here. Might as well put them to some use."

Lily teased to be let down. When I released her, she toddled toward the puddle but tripped on her long gown before she got there. Maude scooped her up. "Now that the child is walking, you should hem up her dress. Two, maybe three inches above the ankle. Then it won't get in her way."

I could feel my face burn. Who did she think she was? It was bad enough her thinking she had to show me ways to entertain Lily, but now she was telling me how to dress her, too? I had managed Lily's care for over a year without any advice from a tavern keeper. And I had little enough time to myself when Lily was sleeping. I wasn't going to spend any of it hemming a dress. "Lily will be fine," I said. "She's very steady on her feet. That was just an accident."

"Suit yourself," Maude said. "I've spent too long dal-lying around. Have to get back to the kitchen, or there won't be any dinner." She handed Lily to me and disap-peared around the side of the tavern.

Lily begged to be let down, then tugged on my skirt, leading me over to the hollyhocks. She pointed and whined until I fashioned another doll for her. Lily wheedled me into making one after another until we had a whole parade of fine ladies moving around the puddle in the gentle breeze. It must have been over an hour before I remembered Joshua.

It wasn't easy to coax Lily away from her new play-things. Finally I had to pick her up, and she kicked and yelled as I carried her around to the street. Then she for-got about the flower dolls and was content to toddle alongside me, holding my hand. Several women with shopping baskets smiled at Lily as they passed us. She was a sight to behold now that her curls had turned the color of Grandma's amber beads. We walked all the way up Dominick Street. I called out for Joshua down the narrow alleys between the houses and shops, but I didn't find him. When we reached the watering trough in front of the big hotel, we turned down James Street. "I should have known better than to let Joshua go wandering off," I complained to Lily.

"Shasha?" she asked, her eyes worried.

"Don't worry, Lily. We'll find him."

Suddenly Lily's face lit up. "Shasha!" she called, point-ing her pudgy finger back toward Dominick Street. There was Joshua, running toward us. I wondered if Lily would ever brighten at the sight of me as much as she did when she saw Joshua. Back at the cabin, my chores had kept me from spending more time with Lily, but now all I had to do all day long was care for her. The only trouble was, since she started walking, it seemed I was always having to say no to her or whisk her away from things that interested her before she got into mischief.

Joshua arrived, breathless. "Mem! You'll never guess what I found!"

"I don't care what you found. I told you to stay right near the tavern. I can't be worrying about you running all over town."

"But Mem, I found the most wonderful place. And nobody knows it's there."

"What place?"

"It's a fort, with a drawbridge and everything. Well, at least you can see where the drawbridge used to be."

"Don't tell tales, Joshua. We walked through the whole town with Papa last night after supper and didn't see any sign of a fort."

"Well, we didn't go that way last night, but that's just the thing, Mem. You could walk right by and never know it's there."

"Stop it, Joshua. Mama taught us to always tell the truth. It's all right to think things up, but you mustn't try to make out that they're real."

"But it is the truth," Joshua insisted. He took hold of my sleeve and started pulling me across the square. He seemed so convinced he was right, I finally lifted Lily on my hip and followed.

# Three

We fairly ran the rest of the way down James Street, Lily bouncing along on my hip as if she were riding horseback, squealing with delight. Joshua turned left on Dominick Street and took the part of the road that headed out of town.

"Where are you going?" I called, but he didn't stop until he reached an open space beyond the last of the houses. There was nothing but a slight rise in the ground off to the left, with a few patches of picket fence in front of it.

"All right," I said. "Where's your fort?"

"There," he said, pointing to the mound.

"You've gone daft. You've brought us all the way out here for nothing." I tried to sound cross, but I couldn't really be upset with him. We had nothing better to fill our time until lunch, what with having to keep Lily out of the tavern.

Joshua grinned. "You just wait till you see." He ran off across the field, up the mound. When I reached the top, I saw that the rise in the ground hid a deep trench with steeply slanted grass-covered sides. The pickets were sharp and tall, half again the height of a man, but so little showed above the ground, it had appeared as nothing more than a garden fence. An old gatehouse the size and shape of a small cabin still stood. Inside on its side walls there was a curved wooden track about a foot wide that once must have held the counterweight for a drawbridge, but now the bridge itself was gone. On the other side of the trench was indeed a fort, though most of the buildings were only charred remains.

"Wasn't I right, Mem?" Joshua's eyes sparkled. "Isn't it a grand fort? And nobody knows about it."

"A town can't have a fort this big without people knowing about it, Joshua. It has simply fallen into ruin and nobody cares about it anymore."

"I care," Joshua said, his face crestfallen.

I put my arm around his shoulders. "It's a fine fort. I just meant that nobody is using it anymore. Maybe there was a time when they needed it for protection against Indian attacks."

"Let's go exploring, Mem. I'd only just begun to look when I went back to get you." He had already started down into the trench before I could answer.

"I can't get down there with Lily," I called after him. "I'll watch her here while you look around, but mind you just look. That means don't touch anything, hear?"

"I won't."

I set Lily down on the ground. "And you'll come when I call you?"

There was no answer to that question as Joshua reached the bottom of the trench and started climbing up the other side. "I hope I haven't made a mistake in letting him go," I said, more to myself than Lily. Then I realized that while my attention had been on Joshua, she had already toddled on ahead of me.

"Lily, wait!" I called, but she only grinned at me and picked up speed, suddenly disappearing over the edge of the trench. I dove for her and tried to grasp the hem of her dress, but she rolled away out of my reach. I watched in horror as she rolled and bounced, limbs flailing like a rag doll, all the way to the bottom.

"Lily!" I screamed. I half stumbled, half slid to the bottom, afraid of what I might find.

Lily was struggling to her feet when I reached her. I picked her up and examined her for broken bones, but she seemed to be fine—not a scratch. She pointed to the top of the trench. "More!" she said, bouncing in my arms.

I laughed. "You thought that was a game? You near scared the breath right out of me."

Now that I was down in the trench, I was surprised at the size of it. A full-sized cabin could be built across its width with room to spare on both sides. I tried to picture what battles might have been fought here. Then I remembered that Miss Becher had told us of a fort in Rome that had been the first to fly the flag of our new nation before an enemy. It had happened during a battle with the British. I had never been much interested in wars, but the story of that flag had stayed in my memory.

The new flag was to have thirteen red and white stripes and thirteen stars on a patch of blue. The general in charge of the fort was so anxious to have the new flag, he had the women in the fort make one. They used army shirts for the white, the cloak of a captured British officer for the blue, and a woman's petticoat for the red. I always wondered about that woman and how she felt seeing part of her petticoat flapping in the breeze on the fort's bastion for all the world to see. I hoped she was proud. I would have been. I'd have to tell Joshua what a role his fort had played in our nation's history.

Remembering Joshua, I called to him a few times, then gave up and started the task of getting Lily out of the trench. I'd have a better view to find Joshua from the top. I tried pushing her ahead of me with one hand while I grabbed at clumps of grass to help pull me up. It was hard to get a footing on the slippery grass.

I was barely making some headway when I heard shouting. Then Joshua came scrambling down the slope from the fort, sending a shower of pebbles ahead of him. He was followed by three boys about my age in close pursuit. I slid back to the bottom, handed Lily off to Joshua, and put myself between them and the boys. "Leave my brother alone," I said.

The tallest of the boys jutted out his chin. "You tell your brother to stay out of our fort, or he'll get what's coming to him."

Joshua leaned out from behind me. "You didn't build this fort."

A second boy, with a pointed nose, came to the front. "We didn't build it, but we claim it as ours. We got here first. If you don't get out of here, we'll beat you all till you run home crying."

I was going to argue that the fort was big enough for all the children in town to play in, but I didn't like our situation. These boys looked mean, and we were stuck in the bottom of a trench with them. It was going to take some doing to get Lily back to the top, and I knew I couldn't manage it with any speed. So I swallowed my pride and let the bullies have their way. "I'm sorry. We didn't know this was your fort. We'll leave now, and we won't come back."

"But Mem . . . ," Joshua whined.

"I said we're leaving. Now scoot." I shoved Joshua toward the wall and gave him a boost in the rear.

The tallest boy, who had been slapping a fist into his palm, itching for a brawl, looked disappointed. Pointy

Nose started taunting Joshua. "Little yellowbelly has to mind his sister," he said in a singsong voice.

I saw Joshua make a fist.

"Joshua, leave it be," I said, and I gave him another push.

The climb to the top seemed endless. The whole time the boys kept up a chorus of jeers and hurled stones at us.

At the top, out of sight of our tormentors, Joshua burst into tears. "Why did you let them do that?" he cried, his face red with anger. "I have as much right to be in that fort as they do."

"I know, but they live here, they got there first, they're bigger than you, and there are three of them. Use your head, Joshua. If they don't want you in that fort, you can't go in there."

"But . . ."

"No arguments!"

"Not even if . . ."

"No!"

"I hate you!" Joshua cried, and he ran off toward the tavern.

"You go to the room!" I yelled. "And stay out of trouble."

❧     ❧     ❧

Joshua was sitting on the front steps of the tavern when we got there, pouting. Lily squirmed in my arms until I let her go to him. "Shasha!" she called, toddling unsteadily toward him with her arms outstretched. He scooped her up just as she was about to take a tumble.

"I thought I told you to go to our room," I said, plunking myself down on the steps next to him.

Joshua glared at me. "I don't have to do everything you say."

"You know Papa put me in charge of you and Lily. I can't have you getting into fights."

Before Joshua could argue with me, a tall, skinny boy came out of the tavern with a broom. "Get out of my way. We don't allow people to loiter on our steps."

I'd had more than enough of being ordered around for one day. "What makes them your steps?" I countered. "Seems to me they belong to Maude Tucker."

"I'm Virgil—Maude's right-hand man. I guess that makes these my steps."

"That still makes these Maude Tucker's steps, and unless she tells us to move, we're not budging an inch."

Virgil came down the steps and placed his broom behind me. "Have it your way. Maude just told me to sweep the trash off the steps." He pushed hard on the broom, shoving me forward.

I had to run a few steps to keep from sprawling in the street. "That was a foolish thing to do. I could have fallen."

Virgil leaned on his broom and grinned, showing a rotting tooth right in the front. "Seems that would have been your fault, not mine. I was just doing my job. Now take your dirty little urchins and move on to somebody else's stoop for your begging."

Joshua put Lily down and grabbed the broom handle. "We are *not* begging." Virgil gave a quick push-pull on the broom, knocking Joshua off the step.

Lily began to cry. I picked her up and turned to Virgil. "When my father comes back, I'm going to tell him how you treat your guests. I wouldn't be surprised if he found us a better place to stay."

A flicker of worry passed over Virgil's face, then he grinned again. "You'll be camping out under the stars if you leave here. What with all the canal workers coming in, there won't be a spare room for any price. Now if you know what's good for you, you'll stay off *my* steps."

We left the tavern, but I wasn't through with Virgil. Right-hand man indeed. We'd see how much of a man he was when Papa lit into him.

We waited for Papa by the American Hotel. It wasn't long before the canal workers' wagon rolled into town. I saw Papa and waved to him. We ran to greet him just as he jumped down from the wagon. He swung Lily up on his shoulders, and we all trooped back to the tavern, taking our places at a long table for dinner.

I tried to tell Papa about Virgil right away, but he was filled with tales about the day's work, so I dared not interrupt lest I spoil his good mood. Every few minutes Papa would look up to exchange pleasantries with another canal worker who had just come in.

"I've never been part of such a grand project, children," he told us. "Think of it. We're digging a canal across the whole state."

"But you'll only be working here for a short time, right, Papa?" I asked.

Joshua jumped in before I got my answer. "How much dirt did you dig, Papa? Is the canal very deep?"

Papa broke off a big hunk of bread from the loaf Maude had placed in front of us. "We weren't really digging today, son. First we have to get the trees and brush out of the way. Another crew ahead of us has marked it off with small flags—forty feet wide for the canal and a ten-foot towpath on each side. This is harder than building a road because we have to get all the roots and stumps out of the way. I'm not sure when we'll be digging, but when we do, it'll not be deep. Only four feet."

Joshua jumped up, almost upsetting the bench. "How deep is that, Papa? Way over my head?"

Papa studied him for a minute, taking his measure. "I'd say if you stood on the bottom of the canal, the tip of your head would barely show above the water."

"And I'd drown, because I couldn't breathe underwater."

"I guess you would, unless you paddled to stay up."

"Papa?" I asked again. "How long will it be before we start out for Connecticut? A few days?"

Papa scowled. "I can't say for sure right now, Mem. You don't need to know ahead of time. I'll pack up

what goods we've put in the room when it's time to go."
He bit off a big chunk of bread and went on talking with
his mouth full. "Don't be asking me again."

"All right, Papa. I'm sorry." I'd looked forward all
day to having him home, and now I'd made him angry.
I could last a few more days in Rome—maybe even
a week, if Papa had to stay that long to get his pay.
At least we'd have breakfast and dinner together. It
was only the middle of the day that we'd be on our
own. I'd have to find something to keep us occupied
away from the tavern. I was used to working all day,
but here there was nothing for me to do but tend to Lily.
In some ways, keeping Lily out of trouble here was
harder work than all the farm and house chores put
together.

I settled Lily and Joshua to bed for the night, all the
while dreading to face Maude in the kitchen. Perhaps if
Papa saw how tired I was from watching the children all
day, he'd convince Maude to release me from our agreement. As I came back downstairs I saw Papa sitting with
some of his new canal friends, but I decided not to say
anything. After all, a bargain was a bargain.

I knew it wouldn't hurt me to do a few dishes, so I
took a deep breath and went into the kitchen. Maude
was sitting at the table, going over her ledger book. Virgil sat across from her, hunched over a bowl of stew,
and a pretty blond girl a few years older than me was

up to her elbows in dirty dishes, washing them in a basin at the other end of the table.

Maude looked up. "I was wonderin' when you'd get here. You can help Mae by drying off the dishes she's washed. Then stack 'em up on the sideboard in the dining room. You can pile 'em on that tray at the end of the table for carrying. There's a towel and an apron right next to it."

I tied the apron around my waist and started drying the plates that Mae had slipped into the rinse basin. The water was so hot, it almost scalded my fingers, but Mae didn't seem to mind, even though her soapy basin steamed as much as mine.

Maude closed her ledger book and stood up. "I'll be goin' back to my customers. Virgil, you finish up your meal, then leave these girls to do their work, hear? I don't want no nonsense from you."

Virgil didn't say anything.

"Virgil? You hear me?" Maude raised her eyebrows and gave him a sharp look.

Virgil grinned. "Yes, ma'am. I hear you."

Maude was barely out of the room when Virgil slid down the bench until he was directly across from Mae. "A pretty girl like you shouldn't have to ruin her fine hands in dishwater," he said.

Mae blushed and giggled. "Oh, stop your foolish flattery."

"I'm serious. Let me see those hands."

Mae held out her hands, letting the soapsuds slide back into the basin. A rather ordinary pair of hands, I thought, red and rough with stubby fingers.

Virgil took her hands in his and turned them over to look at the palms. "Finest pair of hands I've seen," he pronounced.

Mae giggled again but made no move to reclaim her hands.

"That fine pair of hands is supposed to be doing dishes," I said.

Virgil looked at me. "There's not that many dishes left. I think you should wash and dry the lot of them while Mae and I go for a walk."

He came around the end of the table, still holding one of her hands. I noticed she made no effort to get away from him. Seemed to me that Mae could profit from watching how Maude handled the men in the tavern.

"Leave her alone, Virgil," I said, plunging my hand in the hot water for another plate. "Maude said you weren't to bother us."

"Mae doesn't think I'm bothering her, do you, Mae?"

Her answer was just another giggle. What a ninny. "I'm only going to dry the dishes you've washed, Mae. Then I'm leaving. You're the one who'll get in trouble with Maude."

Virgil grinned. "It'll be my word against yours. Maude knows me a whole lot better than she knows you."

"I don't care," I said. "I don't mind doing my own work, but I'll not do somebody else's."

"Suit yourself." Virgil untied Mae's apron and left it on the table as he led her out the back door.

I dried the dishes in my rinse basin. Then I even washed, rinsed, and dried the dishes that had been soaking in Mae's basin. But I wasn't willing to tackle the stacks of dirty plates and glasses that were left. I hung my apron on a rack by the fire, piled the dried dishes on the tray, and took them out to the dining room.

Maude was behind the bar, bantering with some men, when I walked in. I set the tray down hard, hoping she'd hear the clatter of dishes and ask me how things were going in the kitchen, but the dining room was so noisy, she never looked up. I stood there for a minute, thinking about how much trouble I might get in for not finishing the work. But if I didn't stop this trick, Virgil was likely to try it every night and I'd be stuck with both the washing and drying. I took a deep breath and marched right over to Maude Tucker.

"I've done my work," I said.

Maude looked surprised. "Really? So soon?"

"I've dried all the dishes that Mae has washed. That's what you told me to do, and I've done it."

Maude's eyes narrowed as she looked toward the kitchen door. "I see. Then you're finished for tonight, Mem."

As I climbed the stairs, I saw Maude heading for the

kitchen. I had the feeling I might not be the only one who was finished.

❧   ❧   ❧

Tuesday morning we woke to find that Papa had already gone out to work on the canal. By the time I got Lily and Joshua dressed and downstairs, Maude was cleaning up the last of the tables.

"Are we too late for breakfast?" I asked.

Maude stopped and put her hands on her hips. "You see anybody eating breakfast here?"

"No," I said, "but the children are hungry."

"I expect they are. Maybe tomorrow the person taking care of them will get them to the table on time. Breakfast is over for today." She slammed the last of the dishes on a tray and swooped it up on her shoulder. The curls that had pulled loose from her bun slid through some leftover sausage gravy, turning a dark mahogany red from the grease.

I grabbed Joshua's arm and headed out the door. "But Mem!" he whined. "I'm hungry."

"It can't be helped, Joshua. That nasty woman isn't going to give you any food." I raised my voice and spoke over my shoulder, loud enough so Maude would hear. "Even though Papa has paid a high price for our meals."

Maude stopped in the doorway to the kitchen. "Your pa paid for the regular meals. Didn't say nothin' about me bringin' you breakfast in bed."

I didn't turn to look at her as we walked out the door. I wouldn't give her the satisfaction. Was this my punishment for not finishing the dishes last night? I had done exactly as Maude said. It wasn't my fault that Mae had fallen down on her job. I hadn't seen any signs of either Mae or Virgil and wondered if Maude had fired them. I wished she'd fire me.

We took turns drinking water from the tin cup at the pump behind the tavern. Lily's hollyhock ladies had been blown hither and yon, but she gathered as many as she could find, squashing most of them in her baby fists.

"I'm still hungry," Joshua complained.

I remembered seeing some wild blackberry bushes growing along the edge of the pasture beyond the courthouse. Of course Joshua was full of questions before he'd eat any. "How do you know these aren't poison?" He sniffed a ripe berry suspiciously.

"Because we had these all around the pasture in Connecticut. Mama made jam from them. Don't you remember?"

I watched him squint, as if trying to conjure up an image of Mama, but he only shrugged. He had lost her face already. How I wished I were artistic, so I could make a drawing of Mama for him and Lily while I could still see her clearly in my own mind.

We ate our fill of berries, and I spent a good deal of time washing the purple juice from Lily's hands and face in the small stream that ran through the pasture. I made an attempt to wash out the stains on her dress, but they stayed fast. The purple splotches, along with some green grass stains, almost looked like a fancy chintz print of lilacs and leaves—something a rich lady might choose for her bedroom curtains.

I made sure we were back to the tavern in plenty of time for lunch, but Maude served us last anyway. I peeked in the kitchen, looking for Virgil and Mae, but didn't see them. After lunch I let Joshua go off to play, but he had to swear on our mother's grave that he'd stay away from the fort. I went outside with Lily, letting her turn in circles until she got dizzy and fell down laughing. She soon tired herself out, giving me some peace and quiet.

I noticed that the hem of my dress had become threadbare in places, and when I examined my sleeves, I could nearly see through the fabric at the elbows. Mama would have known how to take some material from the skirt to make patches, but I knew I'd make a mess of it if I tried. Even though Papa was making good money, I was sure he'd not give me money for a new store-bought dress. I was glad we were heading home soon. One of my aunts would either mend this dress or let me have a hand-me-down.

ஒ    ஒ    ஒ

Papa's wagon was so late getting in Tuesday afternoon, I was afraid we'd miss dinner. We were waiting as

usual by the watering trough at the American Hotel.
"What kept you so long, Papa?" I asked when he finally
arrived.

"We're working farther out of town now, and the
hours will be longer. They've built a canal workers'
camp, so we'll be staying there from now on."

I couldn't believe it. We wouldn't have to put up with
Maude for another day. "Oh, Papa, I'm so glad. We miss
you during the day, and Maude doesn't like us. She
wouldn't give us any breakfast this morning, and at
lunch we had to wait till the very last, after everyone
else was served. Some people were leaving the dining
room before we even got our food. I wouldn't be surprised if she scraped the leavings from other people's
plates onto ours."

"I'm paying good money for your meals. I'll see to
this." He went to talk to her as soon as we reached the
tavern. It wouldn't matter what Maude thought, because
we wouldn't have to eat our meals here anymore, but
I was glad Papa was giving her an upbraiding
anyway. Maude glanced at me over Papa's shoulder,
and I scowled at her. I didn't have to be afraid of her
now, because I wouldn't have to work for her. It was a
wonder she could keep any help at all, the way she
ordered people about.

Papa came back and took his seat at the table. "Well,
you'll not be having a problem with her making you
wait until last to eat again. As for the breakfast, she said

you didn't get downstairs until after she finished serving. That's your fault, Mem. She can't be fixing special meals for you. Make sure you're on time from now on."

"But Papa. It doesn't matter because we won't be eating here anymore."

Papa wiped his face with his napkin. "Where else would you eat?"

"At the camp. You said we'd be staying at the canal workers' camp from now on."

"I meant *I'll* be staying at the camp. It's just for workers, not their families."

"But you're not working that far out of town, are you, Papa? Couldn't you come back each night for dinner and stay here?"

"It's not so much the distance, Mem. We're going to be working fourteen hours a day now. They'll wake us half an hour before sunrise, and we'll work until sunset. And the sort of fare that's served here could satisfy a traveler, but it won't give a canal worker the strength he needs to get through the day. We've demanded beef, pork, and mutton at every meal, and they're going to give it to us. Besides, we don't pay to stay at the camp. I'd be foolish to pay to stay here when I have free lodging there."

I must have looked disappointed because he reached over and squeezed my hand. "It's only for during the week, Mem. Sundays I'll be home with you children."

"Sundays! How many Sundays, Papa? I thought we were just going to be here for a week. Grandma will be worried if we take too long getting home. She'll think something happened to us."

"That's enough," Papa said, standing up. He motioned for the new serving girl to bring him a tankard of ale. "We're not having any more discussions about when we depart for Connecticut. I'm going to write to your grandmother again and tell her we're staying a bit longer in Rome. I want you to take the children up to bed now."

When the girl handed him the ale, he carried it to a table of canal workers—the ones he had spoken to earlier. He settled in with them, and whatever he said made laughter spread around the table. He never looked back at us. It was as if his family didn't exist anymore.

I wiped Lily's face and hands. "Come, Joshua. Papa wants us to go to our room now."

"But couldn't we just . . ."

"No," I snapped, letting my anger at Papa spill over on him. "I want you to come with us right now."

When I opened the door to our room, the blast of heat hit me in the face. Lily started wailing the minute I took her inside.

I left the door to the hallway open, even though no air was stirring out there, either. Then I changed Lily and rinsed a cloth in the water from our pitcher to wash her. "Come over by the window, Lily. It's cooler here." Her curls were so damp around her face, her hair looked brown. I rinsed the cloth again and held it to her forehead and the back of her neck. Soon her wails died to a whimper, and when I folded a quilt for her to lie on in front of the window, she closed her eyes and drifted off to sleep. Joshua had stripped down to his britches and had dunked his whole head in the washbasin when I wasn't looking. The water was running down his back and onto the bedclothes.

"Mind your dripping, Joshua. If you soak the bed, you'll have to sleep in it."

"It's too hot in here, Mem. Can't we go outside until the sun goes down?"

"Not tonight, Joshua. Papa will be angry if we don't obey his orders. But when he's not here, we'll do things my way." I knew if we were to survive more than the few days I'd planned on, I'd have to make some changes. And I knew the first change I needed to make.

As soon as Joshua was asleep, I went downstairs to the kitchen. Maude had the new girl doing the dishes, and Virgil was nowhere to be found.

Maude looked up. "It's about time you got here. This is Abby. She's washin'. You're dryin'."

Abby sniffed, and I realized she was crying. "Nobody said nothin' about me washin' dishes."

"You were hired for kitchen work," Maude said. "What in tarnation did you expect to be doin'?"

Abby let out a wail and started crying in earnest. "Not this!"

Maude sighed. "I swear it's nigh onto impossible to hire good help. Mem, you do the washin', then, before we're up to our necks in dirty dishes." She started for the dining room.

"But that's what I wanted to talk to you about."

Maude turned in the doorway. "Make it quick. I have customers out there, and I can't be in two places at once."

"My father is going to be staying at the canal site from now on. Since you were giving us a better price because of my kitchen work, I thought . . ."

Her sharp look stopped me. "You thought what?"

I cleared my throat. "I thought it might not be necessary for me to work anymore."

Maude put her hands on her hips. "Oh, you did, did you? Well, your father and I have already talked about that. We worked out a new agreement. I'm giving your father a better price, but we didn't say nothin' about you givin' up your job. Besides, I need you more than ever now. I've been goin' through a string of bad workers lately." She looked at Abby, who started a new bout of wailing.

"I want to talk to my father," I said. "I think there's been a misunderstanding."

Maude stepped aside. "Do as you please."

I went to the table where Papa was drinking with his friends. He looked up. "I thought I sent you children upstairs."

"About my kitchen work . . . ," I started.

Papa nodded. "I forgot about that. Yes, of course. Go do your work."

"But I thought now that you weren't going to be staying here, the board would be cheaper, so I wouldn't have to . . ."

Papa stood up and led me by the arm to the far corner of the dining room. "You know we don't discuss our affairs in front of others. You should wait until we're alone."

"But I never get a chance to see you alone, Papa. Especially now that you'll be gone all week. I was only working because the room and board cost too much, but now that you're not here, we should be able to afford it."

Papa put his arm around me. "I know you have a hard day watching the children, Mem, and I'm sorry you have to work at night, too. But the only reason we're staying here is to earn money toward our farm in Connecticut. With you doing your part, I can save more of our money and we can leave sooner."

"You really mean that, Papa?" I wanted to ask why he couldn't save our money by not buying whiskey but thought better of it.

"Of course I mean it." Papa smiled. "I'm proud of my girl, able to earn a wage. It's a big help, Mem. A big help."

"All right, Papa. I understand." I went back to the kitchen. If my working would get us away from here faster, I could stand anything—even having Maude Tucker boss me around.

# Four

We were the first people in the dining room Wednesday morning for breakfast. I slid onto the bench with Lily on my lap and tucked a napkin under her chin. It was Virgil who brought our bowls of porridge to us. So Maude hadn't fired him after all. "What a pretty serving maid we have this morning," I said to Joshua.

Virgil slammed the dishes down on the table, slopping some porridge over the edge. "And so neat and tidy, too," I added with a bright smile.

"I'm only doin' this to help out because Maude let Mae go, and then she fired the new girl after one day," Virgil growled. "But it's nothin' to me 'cause I got me a real job as jigger boss on the canal crew. I start tomorrow."

I caught Lily's little fist just before she plunged it into the bowl. "Virgil, they wouldn't make you the boss of a mud puddle, much less a canal."

Virgil leaned over the table, so close to my face, I caught a whiff of the rotting tooth. "That just shows how ignorant you are. I didn't say I was the boss of the canal crew. I said I'm the jigger boss. The one who hands out the liquor."

"What liquor?"

Virgil stood up to his full height and gave me a self-satisfied look. "Liquor for the canal workers. I give each man sixteen half noggins of whiskey a day."

I quickly added in my head. "That's a whole pint."

"Well, if it ain't Little Miss Arithmetic."

The dining room had started to fill up, and the men at the next table laughed at Virgil's remark. I could feel my face start to burn.

"Why do the men need whiskey while they're working?" Joshua asked.

Virgil grinned. "Keeps 'em happy. A happy man is a good worker."

Joshua looked up at me. "Our papa won't want any whiskey, will he, Mem? Mama didn't like Papa to drink whiskey. Remember when she wouldn't let Papa bring whiskey to our cabin raising, and then nobody came to help us build it, and . . ."

I kicked him under the table. "Hush, Joshua."

"But remember how angry Mama got, and she said . . . ouch!"

My second kick made him duck under the table to rub his ankle.

Virgil laughed. "I'll be sure when I make the rounds with my whiskey pail to skip right by your father. What's the name? Nye, isn't it? I'll just tell him his daughter said he couldn't have any."

Joshua's face reappeared over the table. "That's right. That's what Mama would say, right, Mem?"

As I turned my attention back to spooning porridge into Lily, I noticed she had already been giving herself liberal helpings, most of which had landed in her lap. I watched Virgil heading back to the kitchen. Now I regretted mocking him. Would he really say something to Papa? Papa would be furious with me if he did. He never liked any of our family business bandied about. If only I had remembered to tell Papa about Virgil knocking us off the front steps with his broom. Then Papa would know Virgil wasn't to be trusted or believed. But we'd be seeing so little of Papa now, there wasn't time to think of all the things I needed to tell him.

I spent the next few days worrying about what Papa would say when he came home on Sunday. I kept Lily with me most of the time, but I let Joshua have a little more freedom to come and go on his own, as long as he promised to stay away from the fort.

And each night I had a different partner to do dishes with, because Maude was in a bad mood and fired every kitchen girl but me. As much as I disliked Maude, I was determined to stay in her good graces.

Every batch of clean dishes brought us closer to going home.

❧   ❧   ❧

On Saturday afternoon we discovered that a canal ran along a good distance behind the houses on Dominick Street, hidden from sight by a line of tall bushes. I surmised it was the same one we crossed over coming into town—the Inland Canal. I set Lily down on the grass along the bank. She was getting too heavy to carry all day, but she was so unsteady on her feet, she often tripped in the ruts of the hard-packed dirt road. If she fell here, she wouldn't hurt herself on the soft grass. I had been so excited a month or so ago when Lily had taken her first wobbly steps, but now I saw that walking was a mixed blessing. Lily had been easier to care for when she stayed on all fours and easier still when I could tuck her in her cradle and she would stay put. It seemed babies got harder to handle each day.

"Is this the canal Papa is digging?" Joshua asked. It was about the hundredth question he had asked me that day. I was ready to send him off just to avoid his constant queries.

"Don't be a ninny, Joshua. You can't be digging in a canal that's full of water. Besides, the canal Papa is working on is farther south of town. That's why he has to stay there all week."

"Well, then, where do they get the water after they dig a canal?"

"They probably connect it to a stream or river to fill it up." Lily had got herself too close to the edge of the bank, so I picked her up and moved her away.

"Well, then, when they dig out that last bit between the river and the canal, the men doing the digging would get swept away by all the water, wouldn't they?"

I wasn't about to admit to Joshua that I didn't have any idea where the water would come from. It was hard enough to get him to obey me without him finding out that I didn't know everything.

Joshua squinted into the sun as he studied the canal in each direction. I could see another question forming in his mind. "Well, then, if they had a perfectly good canal right in the city of Rome, why are they digging another one?"

"Must be this one doesn't go where they need it."

Joshua smacked at a mosquito. "Well, then, what . . ."

"Joshua, if you say 'well, then' one more time, I'm going to throttle you."

He frowned at me. "You always told me the best way to learn is to ask questions. You said learning is important. How am I to learn if we can't even go to school?"

"We aren't going to be here long enough to go to school. We'll start up again when we get back home. I don't even know if the school here is in session now."

Joshua plopped down on the grass and pouted. Lily cried out in delight to have him down at her level and crawled over to climb in his lap, adding even more green streaks to her already stained dress. I'd have to swallow my pride and ask Maude where I could wash our clothes, though she would probably subject me to more child care advice than I wanted to hear. I had been rinsing Lily's soiled clouts under the pump behind the tavern, but I needed hot water to get the stains out of our clothes. It was no wonder Virgil mistook us for beggars. Joshua's knees were nearly coming through his pants, and his clothes were too small to cover his wrists and ankles.

While Joshua kept Lily entertained, I stretched out on the grass and closed my eyes. The warm sun on my face made me drowsy. I was so tired of having to take care of Joshua and Lily, to worry about them every minute of every day. I just wanted to get back home where I wouldn't have to shoulder my burden alone.

I was drifting off to sleep when shouts woke me. "There he is! I knew he must be back here somewhere. Let's get him." The three boys from the fort were coming toward us. Two of them carried heavy, clublike branches.

I jumped to my feet and snatched Lily from Joshua. "Hurry, Joshua. Let's run back to the tavern." As we ran along behind the buildings, I tried to remember what color Tucker's Tavern was painted. Then I decided if we just got up on the street, we'd be safe.

"This way," I said, grabbing Joshua's hand and starting up an alley between two buildings. I realized too late that the alley was blocked by a gate. I yanked Joshua around and we ran back out to the canal bank just in time to meet the tallest of the boys. The other two were right behind him. There was no time to run. We'd have to stand up to them.

"What do you want?" I demanded, trying to look braver than I felt.

"We want to throw your brother in the canal," the tall one said.

The boy with the pointed nose stuck his face close to Joshua's. "We don't like you messing with our things at the fort. You was back there, wasn't you? Didn't we tell you to stay away from there?"

"It wasn't me!" Joshua said.

The heavyset boy with a runny nose caught up to the rest, breathless. "Can I be the one to throttle him?"

"We're going to throttle the lot of them." Pointy Nose came right for me and tried to pull Lily from my arms. "Let's toss this one into the canal to see if she floats or sinks."

"Don't you dare touch her!" I shouted, tightening my grip around Lily's middle.

He let go and backed off, but Runny Nose raised his branch as if to hit Joshua.

I pulled Joshua toward me. "My brother said he wasn't in your fort, so leave him alone." I started edging back to where the buildings were, keeping a firm hold on Lily and my other hand clamped around Joshua's wrist. It seemed the only thing to do at the moment. Joshua and I wouldn't stand a chance against these ruffians, and I was afraid Lily would get hurt in a scuffle.

I noticed Pointy Nose and Runny Nose still had their branches. Pointy Nose kept slapping his club against his other palm, and I didn't like the way he was looking at me. He whispered something to Runny Nose, and they laughed.

The tall one stayed close to me—so close I could smell onions on his breath. "You tellin' me that your brother doesn't lie?"

"That's exactly what I'm telling you," I said. "And neither do I." I got a better grip on Lily and picked up my pace.

"Well, what if I don't believe you?" The tall boy stepped in front of me so quickly, I bumped into him. Looking over his shoulder, I spotted an alley that went all the way up to the street. I rammed my knee hard into his gut, and the boy folded to the ground, moaning. "Run!" I whispered to Joshua, keeping a tight grip on him. The other boys didn't seem to sense what was happening right away, so we got to the street before they started after us. I had hoped for crowds of people, but there was nobody in sight. Tucker's Tavern was half a block away. I ran as fast as I could, practically dragging Joshua, with Lily bouncing on my hip.

I could hear the boys getting closer behind us. "Grab her!" Pointy Nose shouted. "Don't let her get away."

I was almost out of breath. Where was everybody? There was no sense in calling out for help. We just had to get to the tavern. I took one last burst of strength, bolted for the tavern steps, and tumbled through the door. Some men sitting at the bar looked up as we charged into the foyer.

"Here, Joshua, hold Lily." I went back to the door and looked out. Pointy Nose and Runny Nose were standing down in the street. The tall one with bad breath was nowhere in sight. "If you ever go after us again," I shouted, "you'll get the same treatment I gave your friend." I watched as they headed down the street, jostling each other as they walked. Now that we were out of danger, I began to shake. My teeth chattered as if I were standing outside in a February blizzard instead of being in the summer sunshine.

I went back inside and sat on a bench to calm myself. "What's the matter, Mem?" Joshua asked.

"I'll be all right. I just need to catch my breath."

Joshua's eyes darted nervously around the room. "Well, then, you think those boys will come after us again?"

"They will if you go back to that fort. And next time I

might not be there to protect you. Now you stay away from there, hear?"

"Stay away from where?" I looked up to find Virgil grinning at me, his clothes stained with mud. "Seems you were wrong about your pa. He'd drink three men's share of whiskey if I let him."

I glared at him. That didn't discourage Virgil. He sat down next to me on the bench. "There's something else you ought to know about your pa."

I wouldn't give him the satisfaction of asking about it, but Joshua did. "What? What about Papa?"

Virgil's sly grin grew wider. "Well, they're digging in the swamp now, and when they came into camp last night, I saw your father walking along naked as a jaybird."

"Naked?" Joshua gasped. "Our papa?"

"Don't listen to this dolt, Joshua. You know Papa better than that. He's lying."

"Bare naked?" repeated Joshua.

Virgil snorted. "Yep. Unless you count a thick coating of black mud as clothes."

I stood up, pushing Virgil out of my way. "I'm going to tell our pa what you said. Then you'll be in big trouble."

Just then Maude came into the room. She was so upset at the sight of Virgil, she didn't notice that we were in the tavern and it wasn't mealtime. "Virgil, you get out of here with those muddy clothes. Don't I have enough work without cleaning up after you? What are you doing back here anyway? Did they fire you from the canal job?"

"No, ma'am. I'm doing fine. They sent me back for more whiskey is all." He looked over at me. "Some of the men is drinking pretty good at night, too. I sold all we had. They want me to bring extra from now on."

I grabbed Joshua and headed for our room. I had heard enough.

෯   ෯   ෯

Later that night, after I had finished the dishes, I crawled into my cot, exhausted. I had barely drifted off to sleep when I awoke to the sounds of shouting. Before I could get my bearings, I thought I was back at the canal with those terrible boys from town chasing after us. Then I realized I was safe in my own cot and the noises were coming from downstairs in the tavern.

"What's going on?" Joshua whispered in the darkness.

"Nothing that concerns us. Go back to sleep. You'll wake Lily."

There was more shouting, then a loud thud and the sound of shattering glass. The clamor of fighting spilled into the street. I went to the window and tried to see what was happening, but our room was on the side of the building and all the action seemed to be going on out front. Even by leaning out the window I could only catch sight of an occasional figure under the lamp where the alley met the street. Maude Tucker's voice pierced through the din. "I'll not be having drunken brawls in my tavern. If you have a room here, then go to it now or you'll find your belongings out in the street. If you're not stayin' here, get out now!"

There was more yelling, then a gunshot rang out and echoed against the sides of the buildings. "I warned you," Maude yelled. "The next shot will hit somebody in the foot. Now git!"

Lily jumped and started to whimper. I picked her up and pressed my cheek against hers. "Hush. It's all right, Lily."

"Somebody shot off a gun, Mem," Joshua said. "Did you hear?" He was wide awake now.

"There was a fight, but I think it's over. I'll tell Papa about this when he comes in tomorrow. When he hears that Maude isn't running a proper place for us to stay, he'll have to take us home."

"Could I just go look down the stairs, Mem? I've been hoping to see a fight."

"You'll do no such thing. Get back into bed and go to sleep."

"I don't want to sleep. I want to see the fighting, and you can't stop me."

As he opened the door, we heard Maude trying to convince some drunken fool to go to his room. "The fracas is over, sir. If you don't get up these stairs right this second, I'll throw you and your goods out on the street."

Joshua slipped back into the room as we heard the clumsy stumbling of heavy boots on the stairs. Then in the light provided by one flickering candle in a hall sconce, we saw the dark figure hit the wall as he staggered toward us.

"Joshua, close the door and latch it."

Joshua slammed the door, but before he could slide the latch closed, the man shoved the door open so hard, it banged the wall and bounced back against his shoulder. The smell of whiskey filled the room.

"You chirren shud be abed," he said, slurring his words. He sprawled across the bed.

"It's Papa!" Joshua cried. "What's the matter, Papa? Were you shot?"

"Leave him be," I said. "He's not hurt. He's just stinking drunk."

# Five

The first rays of the sun hit me full in the face, ending a night of fitful tossing. I wanted to wake Papa right away, to plead with him to take us home. But as I lay on my cot, listening to Papa's ragged snoring, I thought it would be best to let him sleep off the whiskey. I studied a crack in the ceiling and imagined it to be the road back to Connecticut. I tried to remember a map I'd once seen of our journey. As near as I could figure, we had moved along that crack just the width of the narrow cot I shared with Lily. In order to get to Connecticut, we'd have to travel past the washstand, over Papa and Joshua's wide bed, beyond the dresser to the far corner of the room. It might as well have been on the opposite end of the earth. If Papa decided he wanted to stay in Rome, there was no way we could hope to get home without him.

After what seemed like hours, I heard the clanking of pots in the kitchen below. Then not long after, the smell of bacon wafted up through the cracks between the floorboards. Finally there was a low buzz of voices as Maude's customers filled the dining room for breakfast. Papa showed no signs of stirring, so I finally gave his shoulder a gentle shake. "Papa, we'd best get downstairs or we'll miss our breakfast."

He opened his eyes, squinted into the sun, then threw his arm over his face. "Leave me be."

I tugged at his arm. "But Papa, Maude only serves for a short time. If we don't get down there . . ."

He yanked his arm from my grasp. "Stop your nattering. I've been working hard all week, and now I want some peace and quiet."

Lily woke at the sound of his voice and began to cry.

"Get those children out of here and let me sleep."

"Yes, Papa." As I picked Lily up, I could tell her clouts were soggy, but this wasn't the time to tend to her. I slung a fresh clout over my shoulder. Joshua was sitting up in his cot, rubbing at his eyes. Lily's cries were getting louder. I shifted her to my hip and grabbed Joshua's shirt and trousers. "Come quickly, Joshua."

"Where are you going with my clothes?"

"Just come. Now."

He followed me into the hall, and I closed the door

behind us. "Mem," he whined. "I can't go outside in my drawers."

"You're not going outside. Here, get dressed."

Joshua sat down to pull on his trousers. His face still showed creases from the bedclothes, and a hunk of his hair stood straight up on top like a rooster's comb. An older couple came out of one of the rooms and stepped over Joshua to get to the stairs. The woman wrinkled her nose as if she smelled something nasty.

Then I realized that Lily's clouts were more than just soggy. I carried her outside to the water pump, with Joshua trailing along behind me. It took a while to clean her up, because Lily screeched at the touch of the cold water, but I knew I'd disturb Papa if I went back to get the washbasin to fill with warm water from the kitchen. I rinsed out the dirty clout as well as I could under the pump, then hung it on some bushes to dry.

We slipped into the dining room just at the end of breakfast. Joshua about drove me daft with his questions.

"Why was Papa so mean this morning?"

"He's just tired."

"Well, then, won't he be hungry without his breakfast?"

"I'm sure he won't starve by missing one meal."

"Well, then, is he going to sleep all day?"

"Probably not."

"Well, then, why can't we wake him up?"

"I want him to be in a good mood later when I try to convince him to leave here."

"Oh." That answer kept Joshua quietly chewing long enough for me to eat one piece of bacon.

"Well, then, why does he smell so funny?"

"You don't smell like a flower yourself. You've finished your breakfast. Why don't you go off and play for a while?"

Joshua got his stubborn look on his face until he realized I had asked him to do something he actually liked. He grinned and was gone without a word. Sometimes it seemed his questions were meant just to annoy me so I'd let him run off alone.

Lily and I finished our breakfast in peace, and then I took her for a walk through town. There was an empty rocking chair in the far corner of the American Hotel porch, so I decided to give Lily a treat by settling where we could watch the people and wagons go by. She liked to watch the horses drink at the watering trough. We'd been sitting there for a while when I noticed two ladies with fine dresses and fancy store-bought hats sitting not far away. I didn't mean to eavesdrop on them, but it was hard to miss their conversation.

"Did you hear the din last night?" asked the one in the purple-feathered hat. "Those awful canal workers came into town roaring drunk. Agnes Wheeler said she could hear them coming from way out beyond the fort."

The flower hat lady nodded. "My husband heard they have trouble every night out in that board shanty at the camp. Last Wednesday the men got fighting drunk. The contractors had to go in and club them right and left to get them quieted down."

The lady in the feathered hat clamped her jaw and shook her head so hard, her feathers quivered like a bird ready to take flight. "Animals, they are. And we'll have to put up with the likes of them until the canal in this area is finished."

"If they had only used the perfectly good canal we already have here, we wouldn't have to put up with this riffraff."

I didn't think she was talking about us, but I was suddenly aware of the fact that I hadn't brushed my hair this morning. I tried to smooth it back with my hand, but my fingers got caught in the tangles. I didn't need a mirror to know how I must look. I gathered Lily in my arms and left, passing in front of the women. Out of the corner of my eye I saw them lean together. I wanted to shout, "We're not usually like this!" But I doubted that the women would believe me, or even care.

We wandered around town all morning and went back to the tavern just before Sunday dinner. I went to

wake Papa, but he chased me out, mumbling something about needing his sleep. So be it. He'd miss yet
another meal.

After dinner I took Joshua and Lily outside and we
spent the afternoon walking around again. By now I
knew what every building in Rome looked like. I didn't
even have to look up. I could tell where I was just by the
shape of the doorsteps. Most of the buildings were on
Dominick Street in the block between James Street and
Washington. Starting at the corner, there was the American Hotel and a smaller one-and-a-half-story hotel after
the alley next to it. Then a frame house with a wagon
shop in the rear, two more houses, a tavern and a combination saloon and grocery, the long house with its row
of tall locust trees in front, a saddle shop, and a black-
smith shop. Joshua liked to stop and watch the black-
smith pounding red-hot horseshoes into shape.

Then we'd turn and go back down Maude's side of
the street, passing more stores, some houses, and, of
course, taverns. Every time we passed Tucker's Tavern,
I'd leave Lily out front with Joshua and run upstairs to
peek into our room. Papa slept on, snoring.

Finally it was time for supper. I'd have to wake Papa
now or he'd have no food for the whole day. I ran
upstairs and opened the door a crack. Papa wasn't
there. I finally found him in the dining room, having a
drink with some of his canal friends. I settled us at a

table where I could watch him, hoping to catch his eye so he'd join us.

Virgil swaggered in, greeting the canal workers as if he knew every one of them. He stopped by our table and jerked his thumb toward Papa. "I see your father is forcing himself to have a little whiskey. If he keeps this up, he may learn to like it."

I just glared at him and he moved on, but when he settled at another table, he rolled his eyes toward Papa and grinned at me. Papa finally made his way over to us, just as the food was being served. "Good day," he said, as if he had jumped out of bed with the sunrise.

I saw Joshua winding up for a question and kicked him before he could open his mouth. I didn't want anything to put Papa in a bad mood. Just then Virgil walked by our table. "Good day, Jeremiah," he said, winking at me.

I thought Papa would be upset at Virgil calling him by his first name, but Papa only nodded and smiled as he passed by.

"You know Virgil, Papa? He's been mean to us while you've been gone." I watched for a sign that Papa cared, but he stayed hunched over his plate, eating with his hands, pulling pork off the bone with his teeth. I tried another approach. "He's been telling Joshua and me lies, Papa. Lies about *you*."

That got his attention. "Lies? What sort of lies?" He actually stopped gnawing on his bone long enough to look at me.

"Virgil said he passes out whiskey to the workers all day and that you drink as much or more than the other men. You don't take the whiskey, do you, Papa?"

"Of course I do. It's part of my pay. If I didn't take the whiskey I had coming to me, I'd be cheating myself."

"But what if you asked for money instead, Papa? Six pints of whiskey a week should be worth a goodly sum."

Papa glared at me. "And if I refused my three meals a day every day for a week, which is also part of my pay, I'd have even more coins in my pocket to bring home. I suppose you'd like me to do that, too?"

Lily squirmed in my lap, and I spooned some mashed turnip into her mouth. She made a face and spat it back out onto my plate. "Of course not, Papa, I know you need to eat to keep up your strength, but . . ."

"But I don't need to drink, is that it? You're not going to start complaining like your mother, are you?"

I felt the anger rising up inside me. Papa wasn't being fair. If Mama had complained more, she might still be alive. I mixed some gravy into the turnip, hoping to disguise it from Lily. She took the spoon eagerly but wasn't fooled. This mouthful joined the last on my plate. I shoved it aside, trying to keep track of what food was mine and which was Lily's spit-up pile.

Papa carved a piece of bread for himself from the crusty loaf in front of us, stuffed some into his mouth, and poked me with his elbow. "I'll tell you something, Mem." He chewed awhile before he continued. "You think I'm out there enjoying myself all day? Well, I'm not. It's a rotten job in worse than rotten conditions. That little half gill of whiskey every hour makes it bearable, you understand? It doesn't make it a good time. It just helps me get to the end of the day, that's all. Then I eat, go to bed dog tired, and get up before sunrise to start it all over again."

"Papa," Joshua piped up. "You know what else Virgil said about you?"

"What's that, son?"

"He said he saw you . . ."

"Hush, Joshua," I whispered. I tried to kick him under the table but missed. He was learning to keep his ankles out of my range.

"Let the boy talk, Mem. Speak up, son."

"Virgil said he saw you and the other men going back into camp at the end of the day and you didn't . . ." He started to giggle.

When Papa heard what was coming next, he'd probably be so mad, he'd box Joshua's ears good. I wouldn't try to save Joshua again. Let Papa be mad at him for a change instead of me.

"Virgil said you was naked."

"*Were* naked," I corrected, then blushed, realizing that correct grammar wasn't important at the moment.

Papa raised his eyebrows. "He said that, did he?"

"That's what I mean, Papa," I said. "Virgil lies all the time."

"Well, did you, Papa?" Joshua persisted. "Did you go naked?"

Papa reached over and tousled Joshua's hair, getting pork grease in it, as if Joshua didn't look grimy enough already. "Of course not."

"I knew it," I said.

"We all wear shirts and hats to protect us from the mosquitoes, but we've given up on wearing pants and boots. We're digging in a swamp, mud up to our waists in some places. It was sucking our boots and pants right off. Almost lost my left boot. Had to feel around in the muck almost half an hour to find it." Papa looked at me. "Don't be so shocked, Mem. It's not like we're parading through Rome that way. There's nobody out there to see us."

I realized I'd been sitting there with my mouth open. This wasn't the Papa I knew. I didn't care how much money he was making on the canal. I had to find a way to get us away from here before things got any worse.

But I needed to talk to Papa without Joshua and Lily around to interrupt.

I quickly finished feeding Lily and handed her off to Joshua. "Take Lily outside for a bit, will you, Joshua? She needs to be out in the fresh air."

Joshua frowned and pushed her back onto my lap. "I want to stay here with Papa."

I glared at Joshua. He would pick this moment to be stubborn. Papa motioned to the serving girl. "I'll take a tankard of ale," he said. "And you do as your sister says, Joshua. I'm sure she could use a rest from the likes of you."

Joshua pouted, but he knew better than to go against Papa's orders. He scooped Lily up in his arms. Lily giggled and started tweaking his nose as he carried her across the dining room. By the time they reached the door, she had charmed him into a smile.

Yet another new serving girl came back with Papa's ale. Soon there wouldn't be a young woman left in Rome who hadn't worked in Maude's kitchen. Papa broke off a piece of bread and sopped up the gravy on his plate. Then he washed it down with a long draft of ale.

My mind was racing, trying to figure out how to talk to Papa about going home. We had to settle it tonight, because if he went back to the camp, I wouldn't see him for another week. "You must be very tired, Papa, to have slept so long today."

Papa shot me a look. "Now you're going to be at me for trying to get some rest on my day off?"

"No, Papa. That's not what I meant at all. I'm just worried about how hard you have to work. You said yourself that your days are almost unbearable." I tried to sound sympathetic.

Papa took another long swig from the tankard and wiped his mouth on his sleeve. "I'm glad you appreciate what I go through for you children."

This was the opportunity I needed, but I had to choose my words carefully. "We're grateful, Papa, but it's not fair that you have to suffer so for us."

"It's what a father does for his family."

I leaned forward. "Mama would be so proud of how you've taken care of us, Papa. But I'm sure she wouldn't want you to be working as hard as you are now."

Papa pulled himself up straighter. "I've always worked hard for my family. Always. Your mama never objected to me slaving away all day on a farm, did she?"

"But working on a farm isn't as bad as digging in a swamp, is it, Papa? I mean with the mud and the mosquitoes and all?"

"You mean forcing a plow through miles of rocky soil, trying to get an ornery pair of oxen to go where you want 'em to?"

This conversation wasn't going where I wanted it to. How was I to convince Papa to go back and work on his wife's brother's farm when he never liked farming in the first place?

"You know the best thing about canal work, Mem? You're not in it alone. I have men working right along with me. And you know those Irishmen? They sing. The harder they work, the louder they sing." He chuckled to himself and shook his head. "Some lively songs they know. A far cry from your mother's dreary hymns, I'd say. And they know how to enjoy themselves at the end of a long day. The work is hard, but it's not . . . it's not drudgery. That's what it's like on a farm. Day after livelong day of drudgery. But here, there's not two days alike."

There was such a knot in my throat, I could barely speak. "But Papa, we can't stay here. We need to get back to our family."

Papa drained his tankard, then leaned on his elbows and looked at me. "That's not my family, Mem. It's your mother's. My relatives have all moved west by now. I'm not sure how welcome I'd be there . . . now that your mother is gone."

"Grandma loves us, Papa. She wants us to come home. And Uncle Henry needs your help on his farm."

"You're not listening, girl. I'm not cut out for farmwork. I hated farming in Connecticut, and I hated farming here in New York."

Just then a man came into the dining room and

shouted to be heard over the din. "All you workers who want a ride back out to camp, I'm leaving now. So be quick about it, or you'll be walking."

Papa grabbed his hat and stood up. "I'll be going now, Mem."

I ran to his side and held on to his arm. "Papa, please don't go. I can't do this anymore."

He looked puzzled. "You can't do what?"

I could feel the tears starting to spill down my cheeks. "I can't stay here. Please take us home, Papa."

"You didn't hear a word I said, did you?"

"Yes, I did, and I understand, but . . ."

Papa dug his hand deep into his pocket, pulled out some coins, and slapped them onto the table. "Here's the money for this week's room and board. Give 'em to Maude, and mind you don't lose any."

My hands shook as I scooped the coins to the edge of the table and slipped them into my pocket. When I turned to look for Papa, he was gone. I ran to the door just in time to see the wagon pull away. Virgil Tucker was standing up in the wagon, pouring drinks for the men. I hoped he would fall out the wagon and land on his head. Papa too, for that matter. Someone started up a bawdy song as they rolled down the street. I could see Papa singing along with the others. He claimed to be working on the canal for us, but I knew that wasn't true. He had forgotten us before he was even out of town.

ৎ     ৎ     ৎ

It was dark now, and Joshua was nowhere in sight. I ran down the street calling to him and found him sound asleep on the front steps of the American Hotel with Lily playing at his feet.

"Joshua, wake up! You're supposed to be watching Lily."

"I am watching her," he said, rubbing his eyes.

"You are not. You were sleeping. Anything could have happened to her."

I picked Lily up and headed back for the tavern. Joshua stumbled along behind. "Where's Papa?"

"He left to go back to the camp."

"But I didn't get to say good-bye to him."

"Neither did I. He left in a hurry."

"But we only saw him for such a short time." Joshua looked down the street. "Which way did he go? Can we catch up to him if we hurry?"

I was about to make a harsh remark, but Joshua looked so stricken, I put my arm around him and kissed his forehead. "He said to say good-bye to you. He was sorry he had to leave so suddenly."

Joshua pulled away from me and sat down on the ground, burying his face in his hands. "What if he never comes back? What if we have no mama and now we have no papa?"

"Don't be silly, Joshua. Of course he'll come back."

But in my heart I knew Joshua was right. Papa would come back Saturday night. He'd carouse half the night and sleep most of Sunday. We'd see him for one meal and he'd be off again. We might as well have no father at all.

After I got Joshua and Lily settled for the night, I dried and stacked dishes as usual. The new serving girl was Temperance, which I thought funny, since we spent most of the night washing out whiskey glasses and ale tankards. When I pointed out the joke to her, she didn't see the humor in it. She was a hard worker, though, and we finished in record time.

I was getting ready for bed when I remembered the coins Papa had given me for Maude. The dining room had emptied when I got downstairs. I went into the kitchen and saw a woman sitting at the table, her back to me. She was slumped over, leaning her chin on one hand. Then she straightened up and stretched. She pulled the pins from her hair, then twisted it and coiled it into a tight bun at the nape of her neck. In the dim light from the dying fire, she looked familiar. I was halfway into the room before I realized I had spoken. "Mama!"

The woman turned, startled. Just then a log fell in the fireplace, flaring up and sending more light into the room. I came to my senses. Of course it wasn't Mama. It was Maude Tucker. The warm glow I had felt for a moment disappeared, leaving me empty inside.

Maude stood up. "What is it, child? Is something wrong?"

I fumbled in my pocket and grasped the coins. "No, nothing is wrong. I just came down to . . ."

Maude raised her eyebrows, waiting for me to continue. "Yes? Is there something you need? Speak up, child."

"I . . . just had trouble getting to sleep. I came down to get a drink of water if I could."

Maude walked over to the counter and poured me a glass of milk. "Here, this is better than water for getting you sleepy. I could use a glass myself. This has been some week." She poured herself a glass and drained it in one gulp, then looked at me. "I think the new girl might work out, don't you? Not so half-witted as most."

I didn't know if she included me in her list of half-witted workers, so I didn't comment. I finished the milk and handed the glass back to her. "Thank you," I mumbled. I hadn't realized how hungry I was. I hadn't really eaten much at dinner, what with Lily spitting her turnips out on my plate and me being worried about talking to Papa.

Maude studied my face. "You sure you're all right? Things working out with you being alone all week?"

"Yes, we're fine," I lied, trying to look serene. I was afraid Maude would ask about the board money, but she didn't. Inside my pocket, I squeezed the coins tight in my fist, being careful not to let them jingle.

I knew I couldn't count on Papa anymore, because no matter what he promised, he wasn't reliable. But he had left me with enough money to provide us food and shelter for a week. I held in my hand the power to get us home.

# Six

When I got back to the room, my mind was racing so fast, I could hardly think. Maude had given me a candle to light my way. I set the candlestick on the bedside table and spread out the coins. I had one dollar and forty-seven cents, more money than I'd ever had at one time in my whole life. I knew I had seen a stage come through town the last two Mondays. I just hoped it was going in the right direction. I didn't know how much the fare would be to Connecticut, but I'd find out first thing in the morning. Tonight I needed to plan what to take. I picked up Joshua's shirt and trousers from the floor where he had dropped them. The trouser knees were caked with dried mud. I rubbed at them with the one coarse towel Maude had provided for the whole family and found that under the dirt, the fabric had worn thin as tissue.

I thought of the women who had looked so disdainfully at us on the hotel porch. I didn't want to be stuck for days in a stagecoach with people who treated us like street urchins. Even worse, I didn't want Grandma to be ashamed of us when we arrived back home. It had always been important to Mama that we looked presentable. I had many memories of her wiping dirt from our hands and faces and brushing my hair until I thought it would pull out from my scalp.

After moving the candlestick to the dresser, I searched through our other clothes. There was an extra pair of trousers for Joshua, but they looked too small to fit him. Just to make sure, I took them over to the bed and measured them against his sleeping form. They only reached a hand's breadth below his knee, and they were far too narrow to go around his middle. The fabric would make good patches, though. I dug through another drawer and found Mama's little sewing pouch. It contained scissors, two spools of thread, and a cushion with one needle and a few pins. I cut two patches from the pants, then laid Joshua's trousers over my lap and set to work. How I wished I had watched Mama when she patched our clothes. She had tried to teach me, but I so hated any needlework, I daydreamed during her instructions. Since I had planned to be a teacher and stay single, it seemed foolish information to me. Little did I know then that I would be raising a family whether I wanted to or not.

It took me thirteen attempts before I got the needle threaded. I knew that because I counted them to keep from screaming out loud and waking Lily. I couldn't remember whether Mama sewed the patch on from the front or the back of the fabric, but I decided it would be easier from the front. I turned under the raw edges of the first patch, placed it over the thin spot, and started to stitch.

As I worked, bent over the fabric on my lap, Mama's voice came back to me. "You must do small stitches, Mem, so tiny they can't be seen. A woman is judged by the fine quality of her needlework." I shuddered to think of how I had vexed Mama, doing stitches so large and clumsy they could be seen from across a room. But I worked hard now to follow the instructions I remembered.

When I was around three sides of the patch, I realized I had been biting my lip so hard, I could taste blood. I slid my hand into the trouser leg to view my work, but it stopped at the knee. I had stitched the patch through both the front and the back of the leg. As I tried to throw the trousers on the floor, I felt a tug on my skirt. I had sewn myself to the whole mess!

I spent what seemed like hours snipping my nearly invisible stitches from the patch and managed to put some cuts in Joshua's trousers in the process. I had learned one thing in spite of Mama's opinion. When you sew something, which I planned never to do again in my whole entire life, you should make the stitches big enough to see when you have to rip them out. After all, everyone knew clothes were held together by stitches, so there was no sense in making people think you had simply conjured the pieces of fabric to hold together by themselves.

I didn't even consider trying to resew the patches. Joshua could just keep his hands on his knees for the whole stagecoach trip. It served him right for being so hard on his clothes.

℀   ℀   ℀

In spite of my exhaustion, I didn't sleep well. I flailed around in the bed, worrying about what Papa would say when he found out I had disobeyed him. I tried to comfort myself with the fact that Papa had never directly ordered me not to take Joshua and Lily back home. But using the board money was stealing, and I knew that was wrong. Of course we weren't actually stealing the money, since we weren't staying at the tavern this week. Well, we were staying one night and eating breakfast, and maybe taking some bread and fruit from the table for lunch.

I tried to remember how the board was divided between the room and the food. Was it four cents a day for the room? And lunch and breakfast together were ten cents, so that would make fourteen cents if we took food for lunch. But that was figured before we knew that Papa would be staying at the canal camp during the week. It was too complicated. I didn't want to cheat Maude, so I left fourteen cents. I was left with one dollar and thirty-three cents to get us all the way to Connecticut. Would it be enough? It would have to be. I went back to bed to toss some more and was up with the first rays of sunlight Monday morning. There was no time to waste.

"Get up, Joshua. I need to wash your hair."

Joshua squinted at me and rolled over to face the wall. I tugged at his shoulder. "Wake up. We're going to take a stagecoach to Connecticut today."

That pulled him out of his slumber. "A stagecoach? Is Papa here?" He sat on the edge of the bed, rubbing his eyes.

"No, we're going by ourselves. Just you and me and Lily."

Joshua's eyes grew wide. "Really? How soon will Papa come after us?"

"I don't know. But I do know that they'll not let you on a stagecoach looking like this." I pulled him across the room and made him dunk his head in the wash-basin.

"Stop, Mem, it's cold!"

He tried to stand up, but I held his head in the basin with one hand and scrubbed with the other. "Hold still. I'm just going to get the worst of the dirt out. I wish I had some soap." Joshua continued to struggle, so I gave up and threw the towel over his head.

I put Lily in her blue dress, the least stained of the two. After we all had our breakfast, I left Lily in Joshua's care and went to find out about the stagecoach. I had seen it stop at the American Hotel, so I went there to inquire.

"Is this the proper place to buy stagecoach tickets?" I asked the clerk behind the counter.

"That it is. There's a coach to Utica departing in an hour."

"It just goes to Utica?" I asked.

The man nodded. "You can get a coach to Albany from there."

I couldn't believe my luck. We'd be able to leave right away. "How long does it take to get to Connecticut?"

"Connecticut is a big state. Where you trying to get to?"

"Hartland."

The clerk shook his head. "Never heard of it." He opened a book on the counter and ran his finger down the page. "What's it near? Hartford, maybe?"

I remembered the trips we had taken to Hartford. It was probably a day's walk from home, but if that was the closest we could get, I'd have to take it. I'd worry about the rest of the trip when we got there. "Yes, thank you, Hartford would be fine."

"It's two days to Albany, another day and a half to Hartford."

Only three and a half days until we got to Grandma's. What a wonder this modern transportation was. I'd seen stagecoaches pass us on our trip to the Genesee Country. They flew by, leaving dust that hung in the air like smoke on a damp day.

"So you still want tickets?"

"Yes, I'm sorry. I want tickets for today."

The man went back to his list. "How many people going?"

"Three. Me and my brother and my baby sister."

He looked up. "Your ma and pa aren't going with you?"

"No, they're sending us to visit our grandmother."

He nodded but gave me an odd look. "All right. The baby young enough to sit on your lap?"

I tried to picture Lily sitting quietly on my lap for even a few minutes, much less several days. "She'd best have her own seat," I said.

The man looked up over the rims of his glasses. "You want to pay full fare for her?"

I clutched at the coins in my pocket, wondering how far they would go. If it cost fourteen cents a day for three of us to stay in a room and eat three meals, the stagecoach fare should be less, because we only had room to sit and we weren't getting any meals. But we weren't just sitting in one place. The stagecoach was going to take us to Hartford, so they must charge something extra for that—maybe as much as fifteen cents a day for each of us. That would be forty-five cents a day.

Almost a dollar for the first two days, not counting meals. "I'll hold the baby on my lap," I said.

"What about the boy? He big enough for a seat, or are you holding him, too?"

"He'll need a seat," I said. "Well, maybe not a whole one. He could probably fit in half a seat." I was frantically running numbers through my head, trying to figure if I had enough but afraid to find out.

The man laughed and leaned on the counter. "Well, now, there we have a problem. That's going to leave half a seat empty, and since it's not likely I'm going to get half a person coming in here today, you'll have to pay for the whole seat or have your brother trot along behind the coach."

That thought was tempting but not practical. "All right. I'll take two tickets to Hartford. How much will that be?"

The man went back to his book. I thought it odd he hadn't committed some of these numbers to memory. Surely he must have to give out the information enough times to remember at least part of it. "Let's see," he said, rubbing his beard. "The fare to Albany is . . . five dollars and seventy-six cents."

I gasped. "Over five dollars for two people?"

"No, I gave you the fare for one person. Eleven dollars, fifty-two cents, all told. And then the fare on to Hartford is . . . Let's see." He was running his finger down another page.

"It's no matter," I said, barely able to talk over the lump in my throat. "I don't have enough money."

He closed the book and smiled. "You know, child, I must get two, maybe three children coming in here every month thinking they're going to run away by stagecoach." He reached into a candy jar and set three peppermint drops on the counter. "No matter how hard things are, you're still getting three meals a day and a roof over your head, aren't you?"

I couldn't speak, and the tears blurred my vision. I wanted to tell him we weren't running away. There was nothing here to run away from. We were running home.

"Take the candy back to your brother and sister and see if that doesn't make the day a little sweeter."

Candy! As if a piece of candy could make everything better. I turned to leave and got as far as the door when I changed my mind. I went back and took the candy. "Thank you," I mumbled.

"That's a good girl," the clerk said. "You go on home now and mind your ma and pa. By tonight you'll forget what you were so overwrought about."

The hot sun hit me full in the face as I went outside. It was the first time I realized I was angry at Mama as well as Papa. I was angry that she let herself go mad. I was angry that she gave up and died. I was angry that she left me alone with two children to care for. And most of all, I was angry at myself for being stupid enough to think I had enough money to get us back home.

The streets of Rome were starting to fill with people as I walked back to the tavern. I kept my face composed so as not to attract attention and tried to imagine myself as the girl the hotel clerk saw. In my mind, I walk back to a cozy house and find Joshua playing in the front yard. When I go inside, I'm greeted by the smells of bread, fresh from the oven. Mama is sitting near the fire, holding Lily. She looks up as I come in. "Where have you been, Mem? I was looking for you. I know how you love the first slice of warm bread."

Just as the clerk predicted, I can't remember a single thing about the argument that made me want to leave this place.

"Oh, Mama, I'm sorry." I run to her, but of course she's not there. Nothing is there, except Joshua and Lily sitting on the bottom step when I get to the tavern.

"Did you get the tickets, Mem?" Joshua asked. "When do we leave? How many horses will pull the coach?"

I sat on the step next to him. "The tickets were too expensive. We can't go by stagecoach."

"Well, then, how will we get there?"

I was about to say we weren't going after all when I had a thought. Even though we had come to the Genesee Country by wagon, we had spent much of the trip walking. And I was two years older now, strong enough to carry Lily. Even Joshua could carry her part of the time.

Joshua tugged at my sleeve. "How will we get to Connecticut, Mem?"

"We're going to walk," I said, grabbing the hem of Lily's dress as she slipped off the step and tried to crawl away.

"That's silly. We can't walk all the way to Connecticut. Just wait till Papa comes next weekend and tell him we need more money."

"Joshua, it would take Papa more than three weeks to earn the money for our stagecoach fare. Besides, I might as well tell you this. Papa doesn't know we're going back to Connecticut."

Joshua's eyes grew wide. "Well, then, we can't go. Papa would be angry with us."

I grabbed his shoulders and turned him toward me. "Don't you see it yet? Papa doesn't care about us anymore. Yesterday was the one day of the week he could be with us, but he slept the whole time."

"He was tired from working all week," Joshua said, but I could tell from the way he ducked his head, he didn't quite believe his own words.

"It wasn't from work, Joshua. It was from whiskey. Papa doesn't want to be burdened with us anymore. Grandma loves us. She'll be happy to have us home again."

"I don't even know what Grandma looks like," Joshua said, his eyes filling with tears. "I don't remember anything about her." He put his head on his knees and sobbed.

Lily toddled over to him and patted his leg with her pudgy little hand. "Shasha?"

I scooped her up in my arms and kissed the top of her head. "It's all right, Lily. I'm taking us home. Right now. Come help me get ready, Joshua."

Joshua lifted his head and squinted through his tears. "I'm not going. I don't care what you say. I'm waiting here for Papa."

"Fine," I said. I stood and walked past him into the tavern with Lily in my arms. I knew better than to argue with him. Joshua was getting more stubborn by the day. If I tried to coax him, it would only strengthen his resolve to do the opposite of whatever I asked.

I looked through our things in the dresser and pulled out Lily's other dress and the two extra clouts. It would be hard to wash and dry them on the road, but that was all we had. I knew there should be quilts and pots and pans still stored in our wagon, but I didn't know where Papa had put the wagon and oxen. I didn't want to arouse suspicion by inquiring about them in every livery in town. Besides, for all I knew, Papa might have sold them. He certainly had no intention of going back to Connecticut, so what use would he have for a team and a wagon filled with household goods? The weather had been so hot lately, there should be no problem sleeping outside at night without covering. As for cooking utensils, I'd have no need of them, either. We'd use the board money to buy food along the way. If I was careful, we should have enough to get us through the whole journey.

That reminded me I needed to leave the money for one day's board and I should write a note to say where we were going. If Papa found it and wanted to get us back, he could head off after us, although that seemed unlikely. I took my journal from the drawer and started to tear a page from it. It seemed a shame to mar such a lovely book. I felt guilty that I had written so little in it, thinking that only grand words should grace its pages. I sat on the bed and thumbed through the book. Miss Becher had written quotes from Shakespeare and Keats here and there throughout the book and occasionally a note of inspiration in her own words—surprises, I guess, for me to find as I filled the journal with my own writing. I read what I had written that first night leaving for Connecticut.

> *We've started back home at last. My heart is ready to burst with happiness at the thought of seeing our dear grandma again.*

And the next night.

> *We are one day closer to home. Soon all will be well.*

Those were the only lines I had written. The next day we had arrived in Rome, and the journal was tucked away and forgotten. Thankfully, there were no entries to remind me of our stay here. Carefully tearing a page from the journal, I began to write. Should I address the note to Papa or Maude Tucker? She would probably find it long before Papa returned. Would she send word to him at camp? I decided not to use any salutation at all.

> *I am taking Joshua and Lily back to Connecti-*
> *cut. I have left the money for one day's board.*

I tried to think of what else to say and added, "We will be walking." Would that make Papa concerned enough to follow? Perhaps. I didn't know if I wished that to happen or not.

I left the note on the end table along with the fourteen cents. Then I tucked the journal, pen and ink bottle, and Lily's clothes into a small basket. "Come, Lily," I said, but realized she wasn't there. I finally found her under the bed, trying to eat dust puffs.

I started to leave, then went back to the drawer and pulled out Mama's sewing pouch. Even though I knew I'd never take another stitch, it was all I had left to remind me of her. I rummaged through the last of our things. There was nothing worth taking—only a few outgrown clothes for Joshua and me. I noticed for the first time that there was nothing of Papa's in the room. He must have taken all of his belongings to the canal camp.

I found Joshua still sitting on the steps. He wouldn't look at me. "I'm not going. You can't make me."

I tried to sound braver than I felt. "Do as you wish, but you'll have no place to stay. Our room hasn't been paid for."

"That's your doing," Joshua said, holding out his hand. "Papa meant the money to be for our board. Give it to me."

I brushed past him. "We need the money to get back home. If you stay, you'll have to take care of yourself." I put Lily on my hip and walked away. Lily reached over my shoulder. "Shasha?" she asked.

"Yes, Lily," I whispered in her ear. "He's coming."

I forced myself not to look back. If I went and pleaded with Joshua, we'd be here another hour before he gave in, if he did at all. The stagecoach was just loading as we went by. Good. If there was any doubt which way to go at the edge of town, I could wait for the stagecoach to pass and show the way.

"Shasha come?" Lily whined in my ear.

"Yes, he will. Just be patient."

When we got to the corner of James Street, I put Lily down and pretended to tie my shoe. That gave me an upside-down view of Joshua, hands in pockets, kicking stones in the road in front of the tavern. I couldn't leave him here, but if I went back to cajole him, he'd never mind another thing I said. I couldn't have him fighting me all the way to Connecticut. I picked Lily up and started off down the street. It was only half a block before we would be out of sight of the tavern. I listened for Joshua's call, telling me to wait, but there was none.

Then Lily squealed, "Shasha!"

I smiled. "I told you he'd come."

# Seven

I could feel Joshua catching up, but I didn't say anything. Better to allow him to sulk for a while. At least I knew he was with us.

When we reached the fort at the edge of town, Lily suddenly became upset and cried, "Shasha!"

I was afraid he'd run off when we got to the fort. He'd probably hide and make me go look for him. I slowed a bit but kept going.

Lily giggled. "Shasha peek."

Carrying Lily was as good as holding up a mirror to look over my shoulder. I could picture Joshua leaning out from the entrance of the fort to watch our progress. I picked up my pace.

"He come Shasha!" Lily crooned, and I knew I had won my first battle. Through Lily's "reports" I learned that Joshua was hanging back, sometimes hiding behind a tree, then sprinting to catch up again. I didn't actually see him until I turned around at the sound of an approaching wagon. He had moved off the road to make room for the wagon, but he didn't even look up as it passed. That's when I saw that the wagon driver was Virgil. I slipped behind a tree, not wanting him to see us and ask what we were doing outside of town. I knew he must be heading for the canal site. I wondered if he would see Papa there, and I felt a little pang of jealousy.

"Do you know where you're going?" Joshua asked, catching up to us.

"Of course," I said. I had learned the way by eavesdropping on travelers in the tavern. We would take the road southeast to Utica, where we would find the Seneca Turnpike and follow it along the Mohawk River until it merged with the Great Western Turnpike into Albany. I wasn't sure where to go from there, but I would find out by the time we reached Albany.

"Well, then, *how* do you know?" Joshua insisted.

"I just do."

"Well, then, what happens if you're wrong and we end up in a place with nothing but wild animals? Wolves and bears."

"There won't be any wild animals," I said, striding ahead with confidence.

"Well, then, that's just not sensible," Joshua shouted. "Everything out here is full of wild animals. So you're lying, and you're not telling the truth about knowing where you're going, either. Are you?"

I turned to find him planted in the center of the road, feet apart, arms folded.

"Me wan Shasha," Lily whined. She struggled so hard in my arms, I had to let her go. She toddled unsteadily to Joshua and he swooped her up.

"All right," I said. "You may carry Lily for a while."

"I will," Joshua said. "I'll carry her back to the tavern and wait for Papa."

We stood staring at each other for a few minutes. Joshua tried to look fierce, in spite of the fact that Lily was giggling and poking her fat little finger up his nose. I let out a deep sigh. "All right, Joshua. You win."

Joshua's eyes widened. "I do?"

"Yes. I give up battling you. You and Lily may go back if you like. I won't stop you."

"You won't?"

"I don't know where you'll stay, though, since our room hasn't been paid for."

Joshua looked worried at first, then a smug smile spread over his face. "Maude Tucker knows that Papa works for the canal company. If I talk to her, she'll give us the room and meals and Papa can pay her when he gets back. And just as soon as Papa catches up to you, you'll get a licking for sure."

I had a feeling Joshua just might be able to talk Maude Tucker into writing the sum in her ledger book until Papa could pay. Joshua had inherited Papa's ability to charm people into doing what he wanted. He was also getting too smart to fool easily. But I was older and still smarter. I fumbled around in my basket, pulled out Lily's clean clouts, and tossed them over his shoulder. "You'll need these to change Lily. You'll have to wash out the stinky ones under the pump behind the tavern."

"Papa can do that," Joshua said, wrinkling his nose.

"Suit yourself. But Lily will be smelling like a hog pen on a rainy day by tomorrow. I have to get going. The day is half over, and I want to be in the next town by dark." I kissed Lily on the cheek, but when I tried to do the same to Joshua, he jerked his head out of my reach.

"Bye-bye," Lily crooned, waving her fingers at me.

I turned away and had barely taken a dozen steps when Joshua called out, "Mem! Wait. I think Lily should go with you." He ran to me and placed Lily in my arms, then stuffed the clouts into the basket.

"Shasha!" Lily shrieked, wiggling free again to follow him.

"No, you stay with Mem." He deftly sidestepped her attempt to grab him around the knees. She toddled after him, then tripped, smashing down hard on her chin. She was silent for a second, then turned red in the face and let out a howl that could have been heard clear back in Rome. We both ran to her. When I picked her up, her lower lip was all bloody. "I hope you're satisfied," I said to Joshua.

"Is she all right?"

"I don't know. If she'd stop thrashing around, maybe I could see."

"Well, then, should we take her back to the doctor in town?"

I knew once we got back to town, it would be harder to leave. For one thing, we would be calling attention to ourselves. And somebody might figure out that we had tried to run away and tell Papa. If I thought that would make Papa take us home, I wouldn't mind, but I was reasonably sure it would just mean he'd have us watched more closely so we wouldn't run off again. Probably by Maude Tucker. I wondered how much he'd have to pay her for that.

I rocked Lily in my arms until she stopped wailing and let me look in her mouth. I dabbed away at the blood with the hem of my petticoat until I could see what had happened. "It's not serious. She just bit down on her lip. It's little more than a nick." I blotted at the cut a few more minutes until the bleeding stopped altogether. "We have to get started now, Joshua. You can see that Lily needs you, so it's not going to work for you to leave us. You have to come along."

"All right," he said, taking her from me. "I won't leave you, Lily."

Lily took a shivery little breath and smiled through her tears. She reached up and patted Joshua's cheek. I felt a pang of jealousy as I watched them go on ahead of me. I was the one who had cared for Lily from the day she was born, when Mama was losing her mind and couldn't remember to nurse her. In fact, nursing was the only thing I hadn't been able to do for Lily. I had cuddled her and kept her clean and warm. It amazed me to think that I had kept her alive and healthy through her first year—a period that many newborns didn't survive.

But Joshua had been the one to play with her, something I seldom had the time for, considering all the other chores to be done around the cabin. And now I saw the cost of being the responsible one. Lily looked to Joshua with adoration and merely tolerated me. But that adoration was working in my favor now. Joshua enjoyed Lily but didn't want to be burdened by her care, especially the part about changing Lily's clouts. In that way he was somewhat like Papa. Once I had family around me to help care for Lily, I'd be able to spend more time playing with her than worrying about her. Then maybe her face would light up as much to the sight of me as to Joshua.

We hadn't made much more progress when Lily started fussing again—not wanting to walk, not wanting to be carried. There was no pleasing her. I hoped she'd fall asleep on my shoulder, but she just thrashed around in my arms and cried. I would have kept going, but I spotted something far up ahead that made me want to stop here. Virgil's wagon was parked along the edge of the road. We had to be near the canal site. I wanted to see this thing that had stolen away our father, but I couldn't take the chance of having Joshua see Papa. "Let's stop for a while, Joshua. Lily needs to nap a bit."

"But you said we had to keep going."

"We'll not make good time with Lily fighting us, so we might as well stop. Sit down under that tree and see if you can get her to sleep a little while."

"What are you going to do?"

"Nothing. I'll just check the road ahead. I'll be right back."

"Why don't you get Lily to go to sleep and I'll check the road?"

"Because Lily likes you best," I said.

"Oh." Joshua smiled. "That's right."

I set down my basket and hurried along the road toward Virgil's wagon. He had tied his horse's reins to a low-hanging branch. The band of trees along the edge of the road wasn't as wide as I had thought. After thirty feet or so the trees ended and I found myself standing on high ground, with a huge swamp stretching out below. A long board shanty stood on what appeared to be solid land at the edge of the swamp. A large cook fire was burning nearby. The skeletons of dead and dying cedar trees stretched skyward out of the black mud beyond. It was altogether the most desolate landscape I had ever seen.

And there in the distance, forty or so men scurried around like ants, some almost waist deep in the mud.

It seemed impossible that they would be able to dig a canal through such muck. Some wielded shovels and spades while others pushed strange wheelbarrows with rounded sides. I started to walk down the slope to get a closer look but was almost immediately set upon by a cloud of mosquitoes. I slapped at them, but they were thick and insistent, so I scrambled back up again. At the high point, I took one last look at the scene below.

So this was the grand project that had taken away our father. I was sure he was among these men, though I was too far away to make out which one. "Is it worth the price you paid, Papa?" I whispered to myself. "Is the Erie Canal worth more than your family?"

A mosquito stung my cheek. I turned and ran all the way back to where I had left Joshua and Lily, tears blurring my sight.

"I'm thirsty," Joshua complained when I reached them. "Do you have something in that basket to drink?"

"No," I said, turning my head so he wouldn't see that I'd been crying. "We can stop at a stream to get some water."

Joshua looked around. "What stream?"

I wasn't in the mood for Joshua's questions. "Well, I just can't produce one out of thin air because you're thirsty. If you'll be quiet, I'll see if I can hear moving water."

This was a trick my woodsman friend, Artemus Ware, had taught me. He had rescued me when I was lost on our first journey and he had come back last year when we were nearly out of food. He taught me that I never needed to go hungry or thirsty—to depend on myself and nobody else.

I stood by the edge of the road and tuned my ears to the silence, trying to pick up the faintest trickle of a stream. The air was so calm in the heat of the day, there wasn't even a slight rustle of leaves to interfere. The conditions were perfect for finding water, but it only worked if there was actually a stream nearby, which apparently there wasn't.

"Well, then, do you hear water?" Joshua demanded.

"No, not right here, but we'll see farther down the road."

Joshua clutched his throat and staggered on ahead. "Farther on down the road I'll die of thirst."

"Tirst," Lily echoed. She clutched at her throat and toddled after him, giggling.

I smiled at them both. At least Joshua was keeping busy entertaining Lily, so he wasn't fighting me. As we walked on, I was keenly aware of the fact that Papa was nearby beyond the trees. Part of me wanted to call out to him, but the greater part wanted to get away from here as fast as possible. Joshua didn't even notice Virgil's wagon when we passed it. He was showing off for Lily.

We hadn't gone more than another half mile when I thought I heard the sound of water. I had Joshua watch Lily while I pushed my way through some thick brush and followed the sound to a small spring. The water bubbled down from the rocks into a tiny pool the size of Grandma's big bread-rising bowl. It poured in a thin stream over the lip of the rock bowl, trickled down through some boulders, and disappeared into the ground. I knelt and took a deep drink from the stream of water. It was cold and tasted wonderful. "I found water!" I called to Joshua. "Come up here and bring Lily." I took several more long drinks before they reached me.

"Water! We've been saved!" Joshua handed Lily off to me and took his turn drinking from the stream of water.

When he finished, I held Lily out so she could do the same, but she didn't understand what she was supposed to do. She sputtered and pulled her face away from the water. "Lily, it's water to drink. Watch how Joshua does it. Joshua, show her."

He made a big show of slurping the water and smacking his lips. "Mmm . . . water! Delicious! Lily want water?"

"Wawa!" Lily cried, clapping. I thought she understood, but as soon as I held her close to the stream of water again, she pulled away and started crying. We tried several more times, having Joshua demonstrate, but Lily refused to drink. Joshua even tried to show her how to sip water from the edge of the rock bowl, thinking that would be more like drinking from a cup, but Lily would have none of it.

"Maybe she's not thirsty," Joshua said.

"Of course she's thirsty. Babies need a lot of water. She's been teasing every day for water from the pump behind the tavern. I must have poured a gallon a day into her." It seemed as if two gallons a day poured out of her, but I didn't put that thought into words. I finally solved the problem by catching water in my hands. After many attempts, Lily got the knack of drinking out of my cupped palms. This didn't happen until after her dress and mine were thoroughly drenched.

When Lily seemed to have drunk her fill, we set out walking again. My stomach rumbled. The water had done little to ease my hunger pangs, though it had now given me the need to find a place to relieve myself. I called ahead to Joshua. "I have to stop here for a minute. Wait for me. And be sure to keep track of Lily."

"Where are you going?" Joshua asked.

"None of your business," I said, slipping behind a large pine tree with low-hanging branches. I was almost finished when I heard a low rumble in the distance. Thunder! I hadn't thought about the possibility of being on the road in a storm. At least on our trip west, we had the wagon for shelter. Now we'd be out in the open. I had planned so poorly for this journey. Why hadn't I thought things through? I should have brought a cup for drinking and a quilt for protection. And I was foolish not to have packed food. Who knew how long it would take to find a tavern? There didn't seem to be many along this road.

I came out of my thoughts to realize that the rumbling wasn't thunder at all. It continued steadily, getting louder. It was some sort of wagon approaching at a fast clip. I hastily rearranged my clothes and hurried back to find Joshua and Lily. Though I had no doubt that Joshua would have the sense to get out of the way, I was afraid Lily might be frightened by the sound, and I wanted to be holding her when the wagon passed. The rumble was almost deafening as I looked down the road in the direction of Rome. Suddenly a stagecoach drawn by two pairs of bay horses burst into view from around the curve. It was traveling so fast, it rocked from side to side as it lurched over the ruts and tree stumps in its path.

I looked toward the east and saw Joshua. He had walked quite a distance ahead, but now he stood transfixed at the edge of the road, staring at the approaching stagecoach with his mouth hanging open. My heart almost stopped when I realized that Lily wasn't with him. "Joshua!" I screamed. "Where's Lily?" My words were lost in the pounding of the stagecoach.

Then I caught a glimpse of Lily's blue dress. She had left Joshua's side and was toddling toward me, down the middle of the road. She was smiling and reaching out for something. The horses! Lily wanted to see the horses, and she had no idea what they could do to her.

I was suddenly taken back to the time when Papa had cut the heavy top off a fallen maple. Joshua had been playing in the hole left by the tree's massive root ball and was about to be crushed, but I managed to snatch him away from the grip of death.

I had cheated death once, but I feared I wouldn't be so lucky this time. I was too far away from Lily to save her from being trampled.

# Eight

"Lily, get out of the road!" I screamed. This time Joshua heard me and saw what was happening. He took off running toward Lily, but I knew he couldn't make it in time, any more than me. I heard shouting behind me, followed by the snorting of the horses. When they got so close I could feel their hooves pounding the road, I knew they weren't going to stop. There was a loud snap and the sound of splintering wood. A large shadow fell over me, and I felt a blow on my right shoulder that pushed me forward and sent me tumbling into a ditch.

There was a great thud that shook the ground, then sobs and screams. I pulled myself up to where I could see. The coach had turned on its side, and luggage was strewn all over the road. Several men and a boy a few years older than me were climbing up out of the windows. The driver struggled to calm the horses, who were still upright but rearing against the harness that held them captive to the overturned coach. I scrambled to my feet and frantically looked around for signs of Lily. That's when I saw the small blue form under the horses' hooves.

"No!" I screamed, and ran to save Lily.

One of the passengers caught me and held me back.

I wrestled to get free. "My sister! She's under the horses!"

"There's a child under the team," the man shouted. "Quick! Cut them loose!"

The young boy climbed under the wagon tongue, ducked to avoid a flying hoof, and unhitched the horses. They bolted for freedom down the road, their harnesses trailing behind them. Then the boy leaned down and picked up the crumpled form.

I broke loose and ran to him but stopped before I reached him. Through my tears I couldn't even make out Lily's shape. People crowded around me, pointing to Lily, speaking words I couldn't understand. I covered my face and sobbed. What had I done? I had taken Joshua and Lily from the safety of the tavern and led them to this? Papa would never forgive me. I'd never forgive myself.

I felt someone take me by the shoulders and turn me around. "Look, child. Look at your sister."

"I can't look!" I wailed. "It's all my fault."

"Mem, it's all right." It was Joshua's voice.

I opened my eyes. He was holding Lily. She was perfect—no sign of an injury.

"I don't understand. The horses . . ."

"That wasn't your sister," the boy said. "It was this. Just a valise is all."

I looked again. What I had thought to be Lily was only a crushed and mangled blue suitcase.

I turned again and hugged Joshua and Lily so tight, she squawked and tried to push me away.

"Lily's fine," Joshua said. "The stagecoach didn't come anywhere near her. I thought you were gone for sure, though."

"What happened? Did you see?"

"The driver tried to steer the horses around you, but he was going too fast. You got hit by a big suitcase that fell off the top of the stagecoach when they tipped over."

The men were now gathered around the coach, trying to pull a portly woman from the window. "There now, Mrs. Travis. Stay calm. We'll have you out of there directly."

"Easy as we go now. All right. On the count of three. One, two, three!"

There was some grunting and groaning, then Mrs. Travis popped out of the window like a cork from a bottle and they all disappeared in a heap of purple taffeta, buried by her ample skirts. The men untangled themselves and helped Mrs. Travis to her feet.

"Well, I never," she huffed in an accent I recognized to be from England. "I rue the day I set foot in this barbaric country. It's no wonder the king set it loose from the empire." She tried to rearrange her feathered bonnet, which sat tipped on her head like a bright bird ready to take flight.

The driver, who had started off after the horses, had just returned empty-handed, probably deciding that his chase was futile. He approached Mrs. Travis warily, and I had the sense that he had felt her unpleasant disposition before. "I'm very sorry, ma'am. This was an unfortunate accident. One can't predict . . ."

Mrs. Travis turned on him. "One can most assuredly predict this kind of mishap if one is propelling a primitive carriage across dirt roads at breakneck speed. I don't hold with such reckless behavior. Did you not hear me ordering you to slow down?"

The driver removed his hat and turned it nervously in his hands. "No, ma'am, I didn't."

The boy wiggled his eyebrows at me. "The man must have no ears," he whispered.

"What was that, young man?" Mrs. Travis asked.

"Just telling these children to calm their fears, Aunt Mavis," he said, grinning.

Mrs. Travis came over to us, wrinkling her nose as if we smelled bad. Actually, Lily did stink, so I supposed I couldn't blame her. "And where did you children come from? Do you live around here? Did you come out to see what all the excitement was about?"

"They's the ones what caused the excitement," the driver said. "Right in the middle of the road, they were. I saved their pitiful lives by pulling out around them."

"You didn't save our lives," I said. "You almost killed us. We have as much right to be on this road as you do."

"You be watchin' your mouth, missy. I've got a team of two fine matched pairs out there running through the wilderness, and it's your fault. If I don't get them horses back, it's your pa that's going to be payin' for them."

"Nonsense," countered Mrs. Travis. "You lost those horses as a consequence of your own incompetence. Don't try to push the blame on these poor innocent children." She turned to us. "Are you all right?"

Joshua spoke up. "I think my sister Mem got hit by a suitcase. A big one."

"Did you, dear?" Mrs. Travis peered closely at me. "Do you have an injury?"

"It's nothing," I said, but I rubbed my sore shoulder without thinking.

"Here?" she asked. "Does it hurt here?" She pressed on my shoulder, and I winced from the pain.

She called to the men, who were trying to right the stagecoach. "Dr. Morgan, would you come over here, please?"

"I need all hands to put the stagecoach right again," the driver called back. "He'll be there when we're through."

"Nonsense," said Mrs. Travis. "That stagecoach won't be going anywhere until you find your lost team unless, of course, you plan to pull it yourself. We have an injured child here. Dr. Morgan?"

The most elegantly dressed of the men came over to us. "What seems to be the problem?" he asked. He didn't even smile. I could tell this man was not like Dr. Griswold back in Hartland, who made you feel better just by talking to you. This man was used to patients far more elegant than me, and he made no attempt to hide that fact. He poked around at my shoulder and arm, asking me if it hurt.

I wouldn't give him the satisfaction of crying out. "It's fine," I said.

"See if the child can move it," Mrs. Travis said, waving her arm over her head. The ends of the doctor's mustache pulled down at the corners as he lifted my arm and moved it around. It hurt, but not enough for a broken bone. My arm had been broken when I was younger than Joshua. I'd never forget that pain as long as I lived. This might be bruised, but it wasn't broken.

"No broken bones," Dr. Morgan declared. "Just bruised, I suspect."

I had to bite my lip to keep from laughing and thought maybe I should forget my plans to be a teacher and be a doctor instead. I seemed to have the talent for diagnosis.

Dr. Morgan went back to help right the wagon, though he looked none too pleased about it. They heaved and rocked it until it finally landed safely on its wheels. It still tilted at an odd angle, and the driver crawled underneath to see what the problem was. "One of the wooden bars what holds the leather strap is broke," he announced when he came back out. "I'll have to find something to replace it, then get it hitched back up again. Might's well make yourselves comfortable. We'll not be pulling out of here anytime soon." He shot me a look when he said that.

"Jerome," Mrs. Travis said to her nephew. "Would you be a dear? Go over to that heap of luggage and find my lunch hamper, won't you? All this excitement has kindled my appetite."

He came back with a huge basket and set it down under the shade of a tree. Mrs. Travis settled herself on the ground and spread out a cloth. She pulled out a box tied with a red ribbon. "Oh, dear," she said, peering inside. "I fear these didn't survive the tumble very well. They used to be chicken sandwiches. Now they're just a jumble of bits." She dumped them out on a plate and started putting together the pieces of buttered bread with the crusts cut off and the thin slices of chicken breast.

Lily began kicking up a fuss in Joshua's arms. He let her down, and she toddled right over to the food.

"No, Lily," I said, catching her by the hand. "That's not for you." Lily plopped down on her bottom and wailed, but Joshua stared at the food as if he hadn't had a decent meal in weeks.

Mrs. Travis smiled. "It's all right. You may all have a taste. That is, if your mum wouldn't mind."

Joshua squinted at her, biting his lip.

Mrs. Travis spoke louder and more slowly, as if Joshua were either deaf or not quite bright. "Your mother, dear."

"Oh," Joshua said, edging closer. "We have no mother."

"Oh, goodness." Mrs. Travis shuffled the plates around. "I'm so sorry."

"We have no father, either," Joshua said, taking another step forward.

Mrs. Travis fanned herself with a linen napkin. "My! You poor dears."

Joshua managed the saddest face I had ever seen. "We're poor orphans, ma'am, traveling through the wilderness, eating sticks and leaves."

"Joshua! You know that's not true." I turned to Mrs. Travis. "I'm afraid he likes to make up stories."

"Well, the part about not having a mother is true," Joshua said.

"Ah, I see." Mrs. Travis looked at him. "I suppose you felt that embroidering the story might persuade me to give you a treat, young man?"

"I hoped so." He looked down, grinding a small stone under his foot.

"I want you to know," Mrs. Travis began slowly, "that I get quite cross with prevaricators. Do you understand?"

Joshua looked puzzled.

"Liars," Mrs. Travis explained. "I don't like liars."

"Yes, ma'am. I'm sorry, ma'am." I could tell that Joshua was holding back tears.

"I do, however, have a great fondness for storytellers. Do you think you might be more storyteller than liar, Joshua?"

"Oh, yes, ma'am," Joshua said. "I'm sure I am."

"I'm happy to find such imagination in an American child. The ones I've seen so far are such a dour lot, not a smile among them. And the girls seem old before their time, prickly as porcupines, just like their mothers."

I wanted to tell this woman that I was nothing like a porcupine, but I suspected I would probably prove her point. Hunger gnawed at my belly. Something told me I'd be much more likely to fill it if I held my tongue. I tried to force my mouth into a smile, though I feared a

mirror might show it t⸻
seemed to work.

Mrs. Travis beckoned ⸻
for a meal, won't you? I ha⸻
for me this morning. And J⸻
and entertain us with your ⸻
orphan children while you eat⸻

We all settled in around Mr⸻
feast while her nephew and the ⸻ers gathered under another tree to pa⸻ around some fried chicken and a bottle of whiskey. Mrs. Travis's hamper also contained a box of cream puffs, which were pretty much a solid pile of mush, but they tasted like I imagined heaven to be.

Joshua amazed me with the story he made up, complete with different voices for the poor orphan children and the snarling of the wolf who tracked them through the wilderness.

Mrs. Travis followed Joshua's every word, pretending to be frightened when the wolf approached and laughing when the orphans outsmarted him. Mrs. Travis clapped for Joshua when he finished. "Oh, I do so enjoy a good rollicking tale!"

Joshua gloried in the attention, red cheeked with excitement, his eyes sparkling just like Papa's. He had completely captivated this wealthy English woman who wouldn't so much as look at us in other circumstances. I was afraid I had more of Mama in me. While Joshua

ut his life without a thought, I wor-
e worst happening at every turn. I was
d obstinate and likely to speak out when I
ngry. I only hoped I hadn't inherited Mama's
elancholy and madness. In spite of Papa's faults, I knew I had to be more like him in order to survive. I vowed to be stronger and more charming. And I knew the latter would be my biggest challenge.

# Nine

It took the driver the better part of the afternoon to repair the stagecoach. Just before he finished, a farmer returned with the team and demanded a pretty price as a reward. This made the driver even more vexed at us for causing the upset. I felt some blame for the incident, even though I agreed with Mrs. Travis that the driver had brought it on himself by pushing the team too fast.

By that time, we had eaten every crumb of Mrs. Travis's picnic lunch, licking the last bits of cream puffs from our fingers. When I apologized for being so greedy, she told me it had given her pleasure to watch us eat. I wondered if it was the same sort of pleasure one felt for giving a saucer of milk to a starving cat. I had the feeling there was more pity than friendship in her heart. Nonetheless, her generosity had more than made up for my carelessness in not bringing food along.

After everything was packed into the stagecoach and the team was hitched, Mrs. Travis came back over to us. "Now, tell me, Mem. The story about traveling was just that—a story. Am I right? You live nearby with your family?"

"We're walking home to Connecticut," Joshua interrupted. "So we really are traveling through the wilderness. The part about eating leaves and sticks is a story, though." He looked at me. "At least I hope it is."

"Is this true?" Mrs. Travis asked. "You're really trying to get all the way to Connecticut?"

I couldn't see any sense in hiding the truth from her. "Yes, ma'am. We're going back to live with my grandmother. My father is staying here to work on the canal."

"And he's sending you off alone on foot?"

I gave Joshua a warning look. If he told this woman we were running away, that might give her reason to send us back to Rome. Joshua caught my meaning and looked away.

Mrs. Travis shook her head, causing the feathers to quiver. "Your silence is my answer. Where in Connecticut are you going?"

"Hartford," I said.

She led us over to the driver. "These children need to get to Hartford, Connecticut."

"Sorry, ma'am. I can't be picking up stray urchins along the way. The company don't allow passengers to get on anywheres but a proper stop."

"That's a ridiculous rule. What could possibly be its purpose?"

"It slows us down to be stoppin' all the time."

Mrs. Travis drew herself up to her full height, which was considerably taller than the driver, what with the extra foot of feathers on her head. "Since we happen to be at a dead stop at the moment, I can't see how taking on these poor children could hamper your schedule. I'll pay their way, of course. Just tell me the fare." The driver had started to climb up to lash the luggage to the top of the coach but dropped back to the ground when he heard Mrs. Travis mention money.

I couldn't hear what they were saying, but I saw her take something from her purse and put it in his upturned palm. There was a bit more discussion, and she paid him still more. I felt guilty for letting Mrs. Travis pay for our fare. Papa had always taught us it wasn't right to take charity, and this was charity as sure as if we'd begged for money on a street corner. But I couldn't see any way I could get us home without this woman's help. We had traveled only a few miles, and I was already exhausted. I hadn't realized how difficult it would be to travel with Lily.

Mrs. Travis came back to us, smiling. "The driver says he can only take you as far as Utica. This coach is taking the southernmost route out of Utica and will turn off to go to Cherry Valley. You'll have to wait for the next stagecoach to Albany tomorrow morning." She handed me a piece of paper with the words *Three paid fares to Hartford* scrawled on it and a scribbled signature. "If you present this to the man in the stagecoach office, he'll give you the tickets." Three full fares to Hartford. I couldn't believe our good fortune.

"I'm so grateful to you, ma'am. I want to pay you back. If you give me your address, I'll send you the fare as soon as we get home."

"No need to send me anything, child. I'll be traveling for the next few months, so there's no way to reach me. I'm happy to be of help."

"I have some money with me." I dug for the coins in my basket. "Please, take this."

Mrs. Travis looked at the coins in my hand. "You'll need every bit of that for food and another hotel on the way home." Before I knew what was happening, she reached in her purse and tossed some coins into my basket. "Come, get into the coach. We're ready to leave."

∞    ∞    ∞

Soon we were jouncing along the road and I under-stood what Mrs. Travis had meant by traveling at breakneck speed. The stagecoach moved so fast, it made the ruts in the road seem deeper and closer together. And the coach still leaned at an odd angle, making me suspect that the driver wasn't especially skilled at repair. I sat next to Mrs. Travis, and Joshua had the seat by the window with Lily squeezed between us. Joshua leaned his head out, watching the trees go by at a speed far faster than our wagon had ever gone.

Jerome, Dr. Morgan, and the other gentleman passenger sat facing us on a bench that had no backrest. The doctor scowled at me. I wondered whether we had taken his seat or if he was annoyed to be sharing the coach with someone beneath his station. With the prices they charged for stagecoach travel, I suspected that most of the travelers on these conveyances must be quite wealthy.

I folded my arms, covering my frayed elbows with my hands. That is, until Lily got tired of her spot and crawled up on my lap. She reached over and grabbed Mrs. Travis's cameo brooch. When I managed to get that out of her grip, she stood up and pulled one of the feathers clean out of her hat.

"Oh, I'm so sorry," I said, trying to get Lily to release the feather, but she had already stuffed the end of it in her mouth, getting it all wet and mangled. I finally pulled it loose and handed it back to Mrs. Travis, but she waved it away.

"Never mind, dear. My hat has more than enough feathers. Let her have it as a plaything."

Lily smiled and settled down with the feather, turning it over and over in her fingers. Then she started tickling me under the chin with it. "Stop it!" I whispered, as if I could keep the situation secret in these close quarters. When I looked up, Jerome was grinning at me. It wasn't long before Lily wanted to tickle Mrs. Travis under the chin. That's when I shoved her into Joshua's lap. Lily stood up and leaned out of the window with him, squinting into the wind and squealing with glee.

"Mind you hold her tight, Joshua," I said, and I wound a bunch of the fabric from her dress around my fist, just to be safe. At one point we were bumping around so hard, Mrs. Travis screamed, "Slow down!" at a pitch that nearly broke my eardrums. It had little or no effect on our speed until she fished her umbrella out from under the seat and reached out to whack the driver on the shoulder with it.

"Need to make up time!" he called back to her.

"I'll not sacrifice my bones for your schedule," she shouted back, and smacked him again to make her point. He gave her a nasty look but reined the team in a bit nonetheless.

Though we had passed little more than woods for quite some time, now we saw a small settlement. I thought it might be Utica, but the driver drove through it without stopping. It wasn't long before we started to see more farms, then cabins closer together, and finally wood frame houses and buildings as we drove into Utica. Stores and other businesses lined the street on both sides. Utica was altogether larger and more thickly settled than Rome. There were two buildings that towered over the rest, a tavern named York House and in the town square, a large brick hotel right next to the river.

"This is Bagg's Hotel," Mrs. Travis said as the driver pulled to a stop. "I've heard it's a jolly good place to stay, for an American hotel. I'll arrange for you to spend the night. We can't have you sleeping on the street, can we?" She admonished the driver to wait as we got out of the coach.

"I'll not be waitin' long," he said. "This should be a meal stop, but we're running too far behind schedule."

"I have some business to attend to," Mrs. Travis told him. "Don't you dare leave without me."

She took us inside. It was a far cry from Tucker's Tavern. It even had a clerk standing behind a counter, waiting for arrivals. Mrs. Travis marched us right up to him. "I need a room for tonight for these children. They'll also need dinner and tomorrow's breakfast."

The man looked none too pleased. "You mean you aren't staying with them? They'll be on their own?"

"That's exactly what I mean." Mrs. Travis opened her purse and put some money on the desk. "Will this be sufficient?" she asked, smiling at the desk clerk.

His eyes widened when he saw the money. It must have been a princely sum, because he got much nicer after that. "Yes, madam. That will be fine."

"Good, and see that they are treated well. Is that understood?"

Just then the driver came into the lobby and announced, "The stage for Cherry Valley is leavin' now. All aboard!"

Mrs. Travis turned to us. "I'd best get going or that fool will depart without me. You children have a safe trip."

I was so overwhelmed, I could barely manage to squeak out a thank-you. Before I realized what was happening, Mrs. Travis had left and the desk clerk was leading us up the stairs to our room.

The room was much nicer than the one at Maude's. There was a huge bed with a feather tick so thick, one needed a step stool to climb up on it. There was a table with a washbasin, pitcher, and towels. Another small table held a mirror and a bouquet of flowers. I could do little more than stare at this place that would be ours for one whole night.

Suddenly I heard a whoop and turned to find Joshua jumping on the bed.

I grabbed his arm and pulled him off. "Stop it! This room is meant for fine ladies and gentlemen, and if we're going to stay here, we're going to act the same." I brushed his dirty footprints from the coverlet.

Joshua fell on the floor, laughing. "If you're a fine lady, then I'm the king of England."

"I may not be a lady," I said, "but I'm surely going to act like one. And you will, too."

"You want me to act like a lady?" Joshua dissolved into another fit of giggles.

"You know what I mean." My look must have told him I was serious, because he stopped his nonsense.

The first thing I did was sit down and count out our money. Mrs. Travis had given me eight English shillings. At twelve cents apiece, they added up to ninety-six cents. Now we had two dollars and twenty-nine cents. That should be an ample amount for our meals along the way.

I spent the next hour trying to make us presentable. I poured water into the basin and washed all of our hands, faces, and feet with the soap. Then I brushed Joshua's and Lily's hair until it shone. I worked at the worst stains in our clothes with a damp towel and soap. Later, when we came back to the room, I'd give our clothes a proper washing so we'd look truly presentable when we traveled in the stagecoach tomorrow.

"Joshua, keep Lily from messing herself up while I get ready."

The table that held the bouquet must have been made especially for ladies to fix their hair. Beside the mirror there was a small dish of hairpins. I sat on the bench and brushed out my hair, twisted it into a bun on top of my head, then fastened it with the pins. When I looked up into the mirror, I caught my breath. A young woman looked back at me, not beautiful, but almost pretty. I must have been staring at myself, because I was surprised to see Joshua's reflection over my shoulder.

"You look like Mama," he said.

He was right. I did resemble her, except for the sadness in her eyes. I was more like the Mama I knew before we had to leave Connecticut. I took a small sprig of forget-me-nots from the bouquet and tucked it into my hair. My reflection smiled at me.

I stood and picked up Lily. "Come. It must be time for dinner."

We went downstairs and walked across the lobby. Everything was so much cleaner here than it was at Maude's. I hoped nobody would notice that we were the only people in the hotel who were barefoot. As we stopped at the entrance to the dining room, I noticed some of the patrons at other tables were watching us. But a friendly-looking woman came over and led us into the room. She brought a special long-legged chair for Lily that made her reach the table. "Welcome to Bagg's Hotel," she said, handing me and Joshua stiff little pieces of paper with the food listed on it. "I'll be back when you're ready to order."

There was meat of every kind, both boiled and roasted, and a variety of boiled vegetables. But there was one item that made me laugh out loud.

"What's so funny?" Joshua asked. He had been pretending to read his menu, scowling in concentration.

"How would you like fried calves' head with brain sauce?" I asked.

Joshua covered his mouth to keep from laughing. I didn't realize that the woman had come back and was standing behind my chair.

"Would you like to order the calves' head?" she asked.

"No!" Joshua said, his laughter spilling over.

The woman smiled. "It's really very good."

"Will the brain sauce make me smart?" Joshua asked her, exploding into giggles again.

She laughed at his joke. Lily, who had picked up the jovial mood, squealed and clapped. We were the center of attention in the dining room now. I could feel myself blushing. So much for trying to act the part of a fine lady.

"Would you like me to order for you?" the woman asked. "I could pick out some of our nicest dishes and give you a little of each so you can try them all."

"That would be fine, thank you," I said. "But no sauces, please."

"No brain sauce," she assured me, smiling. "But I think you'll like some of the other sauces."

What followed was a meal so grand, I was sure I'd never have its like again. There were bits of every kind of meat I'd ever eaten and some I didn't recognize—most with wonderful sauces. I savored everything, feeling like a princess. What a pleasure to have someone cook a meal and serve it to us. And not served the way it was at Maude's, where the plate was simply slammed down before a person with as much care as throwing slops into a pig trough.

Even Lily seemed to sense we were in pleasant surroundings. She kept looking around the dining room, her eyes wide. And she took the spoonfuls of food I offered her like a perfect angel, without spilling them down her dress or rubbing them in her hair. Some of the women who had frowned at us earlier were now smiling at her.

There was something unreal about this night. I was afraid I might be dreaming and would soon wake at the side of the road with an empty belly and rain pouring on my head. There was an old saying—"It's always darkest before the dawn." Mama, who saw the worst side of things, had changed it to "It's always brightest before the storm." Now I knew how she felt. I feared this was too wonderful to last, but I was determined to enjoy every second.

Before we went back to our room, I stopped to inquire about the departure of the stagecoach for Albany. "That coach leaves at three o'clock in the morning," the clerk said. "You get your tickets at the stagecoach office in the hotel basement. The entrance is from the outside on the Main Street side."

"Three in the morning! But how will we wake in time?"

"There's a clock in the upstairs hall that chimes the hour," he said, offering no further help.

When we got back to the room, Joshua and Lily could hardly wait to climb into the puffy bed. I wanted to wash our clothes but feared they wouldn't dry in time, now that I knew about our early departure. I slipped off my dress and joined them in the soft bed, barely managing to thank God for our good fortune before I drifted off to sleep. But I slept fitfully, waking myself with each hourly chime. Finally at two o'clock I arose and dressed, afraid that I might oversleep and miss the stagecoach. I lit our candle from the one in the hall sconce and made sure all our goods were packed in my basket.

I was disappointed that we wouldn't have a full night's sleep and the breakfast Mrs. Travis had paid for, but I was anxious to be on the way to Grandma's. I decided to write in my journal to pass the time. I wanted to put it all down—how we met Mrs. Travis and how she paid for our journey back home. And how she made it possible for us to stay in this special place. I described everything in the room and every morsel of food we had eaten for dinner. What fun it would be to read this to Grandma. I didn't want to forget a single thing.

I must have run out to check the hall clock a half-dozen times. At two-thirty I couldn't bear the waiting any longer, so I woke Lily and Joshua. They both whined about having to leave the cozy bed, but I insisted. When they were dressed, I checked to make sure the paper from the stagecoach driver was in my pocket and that our money was knotted safely in a handkerchief in my basket. Then I took one last look at our beautiful room, blew out the candle, and pulled the door shut behind us.

We made our way down to the main staircase, which was lit by wall sconces. As we walked outside, I heard a horse's whinny and followed it around the side of the hotel. Here a driver was hitching a second team to the stagecoach.

He looked up as we approached. "You traveling with us this morning?"

"Yes," I said, feeling a shiver of excitement about our adventure.

"The office is through that door and down a flight of stairs. You'll find the agent in there." The air was so crisp and cool, I could see the steam from the horses' breath in the lantern light.

I set Lily on a bench by the door. "Stay here with her, Joshua. I'll get the tickets and be right back." Neither of them argued, as they were too interested in watching the horses.

The man behind the counter looked up when I entered the office. "You here for the mail stage to Albany?"

"Yes, sir. We're going on all the way to Hartford."

I pulled the paper from my pocket and placed it on the counter. "I need three tickets, please."

The agent didn't look at the piece of paper. "You and your parents are traveling together?"

"No, just me and my brother and sister."

"Older brother and sister?"

"No, younger."

The man scowled at me. "All right, miss. We aren't accustomed to children traveling alone. You'll have to mind the younger ones carefully—see that they don't disturb the other passengers."

"Yes, sir. They won't be any trouble, I can promise you that."

"And make sure you board the stage in plenty of time for departure at each of our meal stops. The driver can't

be running around looking for you. You'll have break-
fast at Maynard's in Herkimer, dinner at Shepherd's in
Palatine, and a supper of oysters at Powell's Tontine
Coffee House."

Oysters! I'd always wanted to try them. I doubted Lily
would eat them, though. Surely they'd have something
she could eat.

"You have to let the driver know if you'll be wanting
meals at the stops. He blows a horn as he nears the tavern to tell them how many diners are arriving."

I wondered how I'd decide about meals when I didn't
know how much they would cost. We could order one
or two meals and share. Now that we had the extra
money, there should be enough for that.

The agent asked for our names and wrote them
down in a book. "The distance to Hartford is two hundred and three miles. At six cents a mile, that's twelve
dollars and eighteen cents per person. That would make
the total for three fares to be thirty-six dollars and fifty-
four cents."

Thirty-six fifty-four! I felt guilty for letting Mrs. Travis
pay so much for the fare. I should have told her we only
needed two seats. Lily could sit on my lap or Joshua's.
What had I been thinking? And then she paid for that
room and the nice dinner—and the breakfast we never
got to eat. How much must that have cost her? And I
never got her address so I could repay her. It just didn't

seem right. There was almost no possibility of me ever running into her again.

"Miss?" The agent brought me out of my thoughts. "The fare is thirty-six dollars and fifty-four cents."

"Yes, I know. It's terribly expensive."

"That it is. So do you want the tickets or not?"

"Oh, yes," I said.

He looked as if he expected me to say or do something. Finally he said, "If you give me the money, I'll give you the tickets. That's how it works."

I picked up the paper and held it out to him. "Oh, didn't you notice this? Mrs. Travis paid for the tickets. She gave the money to the driver. See? He signed it right here."

The agent shook his head. "I don't know anything about a Mrs. Travis, but I do know that the drivers don't sell the tickets. They do the driving. I do the selling."

"But I saw her give him the money. And he told her all I had to do was show you this and you'd give me the tickets."

"Where is this Mrs. Travis?" he asked.

"She's . . . well, I don't know where she is by now. She went out on yesterday afternoon's stagecoach." I could feel the tears starting to well up. "She gave the driver all that money."

The agent leaned on the desk. "Look, I'm sorry. It appears that your Mrs. Travis was hoodwinked by one of our drivers. Most of them are an honest lot, but every now and then you get a bad apple." He wrote something on a piece of paper, then handed it to me. "If you write to the owner of the company, he may be able to straighten this out for you. Be sure to mention the date and the time of the stagecoach. That should identify the driver. So many of them are coming through here, I don't know one man from another. Not like the old days, when I knew every one of them."

I crumpled the paper in my pocket, went back outside, and sat next to Joshua on the bench.

"Should we get on the stagecoach now?" he asked.

"No." I got up and started walking through the town square in the dark. I needed to get away so I could think.

Joshua picked up Lily and hurried after me. "But if we don't stay here, they might leave without us."

I kept walking.

"Mem?" He grabbed my arm. "We mustn't miss the stagecoach. Then we'd have to walk." He half giggled, skipping along beside me. "You wouldn't want to walk all the way to Connecticut, would you?"

"No," I said, "but that's exactly what we're going to do."

He stopped and held my arm tight so I had to turn and look at him. His face was so trusting, but as I stared at him, his smile faded. I felt for just a moment what it must have been like for Mama when she sat all day staring into space. I could stare at Joshua and I could make the world go away—all our troubles—all gone. Just stare and don't see. Stare and don't think.

I felt a hard tug on my arm. "Mem. You're scaring me. What's happened?"

I pulled myself together. "We have no tickets. The driver wrote a worthless piece of paper just to cheat Mrs. Travis out of her money."

"We can't ride on the stagecoach?" Joshua asked.

"No," I said. "We can't. But we still have enough money to buy food along the way. We'll go back to the hotel and sleep, then have breakfast and start out in the morning."

"But it's such a long way to walk."

"Look, Joshua, we're used to walking. We've been spending every day walking around Rome to keep out of the tavern until mealtimes. I figure if you put all those steps in a straight line, they'd add up to a goodly sum of miles. This is the same thing, except we're really going someplace instead of walking in circles."

"But we were supposed to have a grand ride all the way to Connecticut," Joshua whined.

"Well, that's not going to happen, so you might as well stop fussing about it."

Joshua pouted until we got to our room. Then he and Lily climbed eagerly into the puffy bed and fell asleep as if nothing had happened. I sat in a chair by the window where I could see the passengers boarding the stagecoach. In a few minutes they would start off, leaving us behind.

Mama had been right. It was always brightest before a storm.

# Ten

After an early breakfast, we headed for the general store. I'd not be caught out in the middle of nowhere without food again.

I looked the goods over carefully and decided on a loaf of bread for three cents and a pound of cheese for ten cents. I also got a tin cup for Lily for twenty-five cents. The cup was expensive, but Lily needed water, and it took too long to have her drink from my hands. My purchases added up to thirty-eight cents. That left one dollar and ninety-one cents for the rest of the journey. Lily spotted the jar of peppermint sticks and set up a howl, wanting one.

"We can't waste our money on foolishness," I said. "We have barely enough to get home."

Joshua, who had hoped to "help" Lily with her

peppermint, pouted. "That's what Papa always said, but then he let us get the candy anyway."

"Maybe if we have some extra left when we get closer to Hartford, we can get candy," I said. "But now we need to spend carefully."

Joshua mumbled something to Lily about me being mean and carried her out of the store. The storekeeper wrapped my purchases in brown paper, and I tucked them in the basket. Just then a knife in the glass case caught my eye. I didn't really need it for bread and cheese. We could break off hunks to eat them, but if I managed to catch a fish, I'd need to scrape off the scales. Then I realized I had no way to start a fire to cook a fish. A tinderbox would be an added expense. I decided against the knife. We could survive on bread and cheese along the way. Maybe we could even buy a meal in a tavern once in a while.

I went outside and got my bearings. The Mohawk River flowed through the town right next to Bagg's Hotel. I knew that the Seneca Turnpike followed the north side of the river, so we crossed the bridge by the hotel and started out. I felt better that we were on the turnpike. Now I could set out with confidence, knowing that each step took us closer to Grandma.

The clouds hung low in the sky, threatening rain all morning, but none fell. A stream ran close to the road around midday, so we stopped and had a quick meal of bread and cheese with cold, fresh water to wash it down. It was a lot easier to drink now that we had a cup.

I changed Lily's clouts and rinsed the dirty ones in the stream. Then I tied them by two corners to a long stick. "Here, Joshua. If you rest this stick on your shoulder as you walk along, the clout should be dry in no time."

He frowned. "I won't carry that."

"Pretend it's a flag," I said.

"A flag of what?"

I had no answer for that, so I hefted the stick over my own shoulder and set off with the basket over my arm, Lily on my hip, and the sodden banner dripping down my back. Joshua ran ahead. "Mind you stay within my sight," I warned him. He was soon far enough ahead of us that he could pretend not to hear me if I called. After a while, I wanted to shift Lily to my other side, but it would require too much rearranging of the other things I carried, so I pushed ahead, trying to ignore the ache in my right shoulder.

Eventually Lily made the decision for me. She struggled in my arms, teasing to be set free. Though I was tired from carrying her, I didn't relish the thought of walking at her speed. "Would you like Joshua to carry you for a while?" I asked.

"Me walk," Lily insisted, so I set her down and tried to hold her hand. "Me walk!" she said, pulling her hand away.

"All right, you walk," I said. "I surely wouldn't complain if somebody offered to carry me." I stopped a minute to watch Lily as she tried to catch up with Joshua. It amazed me that she didn't fall down more often. She picked up each foot so far, it seemed she would tip over, but somehow she managed to balance and take another step. She called out to Joshua until he stopped and turned around, then she happily reached for his hand. Joshua walked slowly enough so Lily could keep up. She babbled nonsense to him and he mimicked her, smiling. At this rate it would take us a year to get to Connecticut, but I knew Lily would soon tire of the walking and want to be carried again. Then we could make better time.

❧   ❧   ❧

As the day progressed, the clouds gave way to sun, and it turned hot. In late afternoon we arrived at a village with mostly white houses and wonderful big trees for shade. I recognized it as Herkimer from our trip west.

"Can we stay here?" Joshua asked.

I set down the basket and pole. The clout was dry enough to fold and tuck away. No sense marching around town with it flapping in the breeze. "There's still a good bit of daylight left, but I suppose it's better to stay

here than get stuck in the middle of nowhere for the
night."

"Good," Joshua said. "Let's get a room with one of
those puffy beds."

"We don't have enough money for a fancy room,
Joshua."

"But Mrs. Travis gave you extra money for hotels and
food. There were lots of coins. I saw you counting
them."

"Yes, she did, but I'm not going to spend it on our
first day. We don't know how long it will take to get
home, especially walking at Lily's pace. And we might
need money for an emergency."

"What's an emergency?"

"An emergency is when something bad happens."

"What kind of bad thing could happen?"

"I don't know. It could be anything." I saw that
Joshua's mind was already working on all the terrible
things that could possibly happen to us. I needed to dis-
tract him. "Look, I'll watch Lily while you go explore for
a while. Then when you come back, we'll get dinner
and find a place to stay the night."

Since the weather had turned fair, I planned to sleep
under the shelter of some trees at the edge of town.
I knew Joshua was expecting an inn, and I wouldn't
rob him of that hope until I had to. "Come, Lily," I said,
settling down on the banks of the stream that ran

through the town. "You and I will play while Joshua takes a walk."

Lily set up a squalling right away, so that two old men who were fishing downstream turned to look at us. I picked Lily up and tried to entertain her, but she wanted none of me.

"That's all right," Joshua said, taking her. "She can go with me."

I stretched out on the sunny creek bank, glad for the chance to be alone with my thoughts. I was exhausted from the day's long walk, having carried Lily for much of the distance. I must have fallen asleep, because I awoke to find the sun lower in the sky and Joshua looking through the basket.

"What are you doing?"

"Um . . . Lily stinks. I'm looking for her clouts so you can change her. I want to go back and see something."

"All right. Leave her with me. But don't be gone too long. I'm getting hungry."

"I am, too," Joshua said as he ran off. I wondered what he had seen that he was so anxious to get back to.

It wasn't long before I found out. He came back smiling, holding something behind his back.

"What are you looking so smug about?" I asked.

He held out a fist. "I have something that will keep us safe for our whole trip. We don't have to worry about any bad things or emergencies. Close your eyes and hold out your hand."

"If you think I'll scream because you drop a squirmy bug in my hand, you ought to know me better."

"It's not a bug, Mem. It's something wonderful. Honest."

His face looked so eager, I finally did what he said. I felt something small hit my palm. "You can open your eyes now."

There was a jewel in my hand. It looked like a diamond and gave off flashes of green, red, and purple when I moved it in the sunlight. "What is this? Where did you get it?"

"I bought it," Joshua said, beaming. "It's a magic diamond."

"You bought it with what? You had no money."

Before he had a chance to answer, I dove for the basket. The knot had been taken out of the handkerchief and the coins lay scattered at the bottom of the basket. "You had no right to touch this!" I cried.

Joshua looked as if I had slapped him across the face. "It was my money as much as yours. I thought it would make you happy."

I counted the coins that were left. All of Mrs. Travis's shillings were gone, and we were left with what we had before we met Mrs. Travis—one dollar and thirty-three cents. "You spent almost a dollar on a worthless piece of glass?"

Joshua's lip was quivering now. "It's not glass. I told you. It's a magic diamond. The boy said it's worth a hundred dollars. We could sell it and have more than enough money to go back home."

"How could you be so stupid!" I shouted. "Do you have any idea how much food that money would have bought for us?"

Joshua was on his knees, running his fingers through the grass, trying to find the jewel that I had dropped in my excitement. I knotted our remaining coins in the handkerchief, tied it to the drawstring at my neckline, and slipped it down the front of my dress.

Joshua found the gem and held it up. "You don't understand, Mem. I bought this so no more bad things would happen to us on our journey."

"You're the one who doesn't understand. What you did *was* a bad thing. You threw away almost half of our money."

"But the boy who sold it to me said he always carried it in his pocket for luck, and he's never been sick or hurt in his whole life."

I stood up. "Well, his luck is about to change. Where is he?"

Joshua carried Lily and led me along the edge of the creek to a place where a big old tree leaned out over the water. As we climbed around the other side of it, I saw a boy about Virgil's age sitting on the bank, fishing.

"You sold my brother a worthless piece of glass. I want the money back."

He didn't even look up. "Why? Has something bad happened to you since you got it? You been struck by lightning or something?"

"Of course not. I just want to return it and get my money back."

He pulled up the line on the end of his pole and checked to see if the worm was still fastened on his hook. "Well, if nothing has happened to you, that means the magic is working. And for another thing, that's not glass. It's a real Herkimer diamond. Worth much more than you paid for it. I have lots of them."

"If you had diamonds, you wouldn't be sitting here with a worm on a hook trying to catch a fish. You could buy all the fish you wanted."

He lifted his line, plopping the worm in a different spot. "Maybe I'm not fishing," he said, grinning. "Maybe I like teaching worms how to swim."

Joshua tugged at my sleeve and whispered, "See? He's nice. Funny, too."

I took the stone from Joshua and held it out to the boy. "Take this back and give me my money."

The boy pulled his line out of the water and stood up. He was much taller than me. "Sorry. What's sold is sold."

He turned and started walking away. I ran at him and pushed him—hard. But he didn't fall down. He turned and knocked me over with a sweep of his arm. Then Joshua ran after him and was knocked into a heap with me. Lily toddled over to us and fell down, thinking we were playing some sort of game.

The boy just laughed, shouldered his fishing pole, and walked on down the path. I knew there was no sense in following him. He could give the two of us a good thrashing with one hand tied behind his back.

"Mem, what happened to the diamond?" Joshua asked. "Did you drop it again? Did you lose it?"

"It doesn't matter. It's not a real diamond, Joshua."

"Well, it could be. It looked like one."

Just then, a younger boy came out from behind the tree. "It was just a crystal. There's a place where my brother and I find them."

"If he's your brother, can you get our money back?" I asked. "He has eight shillings that belong to us."

The boy shook his head. "He'd never give it back. He makes a lot of money selling them to people who come through here—mostly to the mothers or fathers, though. The children usually don't have any money."

I gave Joshua a sharp look, but he turned away.

The boy pointed to a sparkle in the dirt. "There's your diamond." He picked it up and handed it to me. "Some think they're lucky. I couldn't say for sure. But you might as well take it, long as you've already paid for it."

I took it from him and tucked it into the handkerchief with the coins. At least it would make a pretty gift for Grandma. And I could see that we were going to need all the luck we could find to get ourselves home.

# Eleven

The delicious aroma of roasting meat wafted out of Maynard's Tavern's door. "Can't we please go in there?" Joshua whined. "I'm hungry."

"Joshua, I told you, we can't spend any more money. We have bread and cheese left. They'll have to last until we get to Albany."

"Well, then, how long is that?"

"I don't know. Three, maybe four days."

Joshua moaned. "We'll starve!"

I let Joshua go on thinking we would be short of food. I certainly wasn't going to let us starve, but he had to know we couldn't waste any more money.

I rationed out the bread and cheese. Joshua complained bitterly about his portion, but he quieted down when I reminded him that he had caused the problem by taking the money and spending it.

We found a safe spot to spend the night, far enough out of town so as not to be bothered but close enough to people so that we could get help if we needed it. I hoped we could spend each night near a town, as I wasn't quite ready to be off in the wilderness. My courage would have to grow soon, because we were sure to spend some nights in the middle of nowhere.

I discovered a good patch of long sweet grass for a bed and the shelter of a grove of young maples above us. Lily and Joshua fell asleep almost immediately, and I stayed awake, watching the last traces of pink fade from the edges of the big lavender clouds that now crowded the sky. I took the handkerchief from the basket, opened it, and counted the money again. One dollar and thirty-three cents. And how many days to go? Ten? Fourteen? I had been foolish to think that Maude's room and board money was enough to see us all the way home.

Even if Joshua hadn't given away the money Mrs. Travis gave us, we wouldn't have had enough. Of course she was thinking we'd be traveling by stagecoach, staying overnight only in Albany and maybe one other stop. Since she traveled all the time, she must have known how much it would cost. She made sure we had enough for two or three days of hotels and meals. Could we make it stretch far enough? We'd have to. I could eat less—just enough to keep up my strength for walking. My stomach hadn't been feeling right for the past day or so anyway. Probably too much rich food. I wasn't accustomed to fancy fare.

I knotted the coins into the handkerchief and tucked it inside my dress. As I did, I felt the locket that I always wore. I took it out and ran my finger over the lily design on the front. That's what had given me the idea for Lily's name. I had been the only one to think she needed a name when she was born. Mama had barely noticed her, and Papa was too busy with homestead chores to think about naming a baby. I named her Lily, and nobody ever questioned it.

I opened the locket. There inside were three locks of chestnut hair. Mine, my grandmother's from when she was a little girl, and one from her grandmother—the first Remembrance in our family. She had come to this country from England on a ship with her new husband. She had been only sixteen at the time, just three years older than me. She was coming to a country where she didn't know a soul. How much more frightening her journey must have been than the one I faced now. I pulled out my journal and wrote.

> *It falls to me to get Lily and Joshua back home.*
> *If I have but one-tenth the courage of my great-*
> *great-grandmother, Remembrance, I will not*
> *fail.*

I put away the journal, stretched out in the fragrant grass, and closed my eyes. Just as I was about to drift off to sleep, I was hit in the middle of the forehead by a raindrop. It wasn't long before the clouds that had made for such a spectacular sunset opened up and set forth a deluge. I gathered Joshua and Lily close to me under a tree, and we huddled together. The young trees offered little protection, and in minutes we were drenched to the skin. When the rain finally stopped, I spent the rest of the night swatting at the mosquitoes that buzzed around our ears. They seemed to spring to life from the raindrops.

෨ ෨ ෨

By morning I was in no mood for traveling, and neither were Joshua and Lily. "The sooner we get moving, the sooner our clothes will dry out," I said.

"But I'm hungry!" Joshua whined.

"All right, we'll eat first." I opened the package of food and found the bread to be nothing more than a sodden mess. I pulled off a hunk and handed it to Joshua.

He dropped it on the ground. "I'm not eating that!"

"You'll be hungry, then. It's not much different from a bread pudding."

"It's all muddy now. Only a pig would eat it."

"Whose fault is that?" Joshua ignored me and stomped the mash into the dirt.

I tried to feed Lily some of the bread, but she spat it out and made a face.

"All right," I said. "We'll have some cheese. But mind you, this little bit is all we have left until we find someplace to eat."

"Let's go back into the town," Joshua said.

"We're not retracing our steps. We've made slow enough time as it is. We'll keep going until we find an inn or a tavern. Now that we're on the turnpike, there should be more of them."

I broke off a hunk of cheese for Joshua and a small one for Lily. I nibbled at what was left. It wasn't enough to take away the gnawing in my stomach, but I knew we wouldn't starve before we found our next meal.

The sun hid behind a thick haze all morning, making the ground steam lazily like cornmeal mush over a dying fire. Clouds of mosquitoes hung over the puddle-filled road and nipped at our ankles and the backs of our necks. I finally gave up swatting them. There were just too many, and they were too fast for me. Lily was a mass of red welts, and she scratched at them constantly, making the worst of them bleed.

I once overheard Maude Tucker tell a canal worker of a plant that could ease the itch of his mosquito bites. Why hadn't I paid more attention? That very plant might be growing alongside the road, but I had no idea what it looked like.

It was hard to find the strength to keep going. The constant walking gave me too much time to think and doubt my decision. Had I done the wrong thing by trying to get Lily and Joshua back home? Maybe if we'd waited a few more weeks, Papa might have tired of the canal work and brought us home himself. What if Lily got sick from being soaked by the rain or from too many mosquito bites? Had I raised her this far only to lose her because of my stubbornness? A child her age could seem healthy one day and be buried the next.

And what of Maude Tucker? Had I misjudged her? If I had been nicer to her, would she have been more friendly toward us? That one night, when I had mistaken her for Mama in the kitchen, she had shown a flicker of real concern for me. If I had confided in her then, would she have treated me with kindness?

Maude had taken a real interest in Lily. I had resented her for meddling in our affairs, but I had to admit she had given me good advice. I had been too prideful to accept it gracefully. I had ample time to replay the scenes of my confrontations with Maude in my mind as we trudged along.

Lily soon tired of being carried and wanted to walk again, but she refused to hold my hand. The road was so rutted that she tumbled every few steps on the uneven ground. After her third fall I tried to pick her up, but she went all limp so I couldn't get a grip on her. When I finally got her up on my hip, she let out a howl and threw herself backward. I would have lost her altogether if I hadn't grabbed a bunch of her dress.

Joshua, who had been walking a considerable distance ahead, turned at the sound of Lily's cries and came running back. "What's happened to Lily?"

"Nothing," I said. "She's just being ornery."

"Well, then, what did you do to her?"

Before I could speak, Lily reached out to Joshua. "Shasha!" she sobbed. "Me wan Shasha!"

"Fine," I said, shoving her into his arms. "You're welcome to her."

Joshua took off ahead of me, crooning to Lily. I could hear her giggling every now and then. At this point I didn't care that Lily liked him best. It was much easier walking without having to carry her. I renewed my resolve never to marry and have children. Raising a child was the hardest job of all, and you didn't even get paid for doing it.

Just as I began to think we might all die of starvation, we came around a bend in the road and found a busy tavern. Four wagons and a stagecoach were tied to trees, and people were milling around outside.

"Finally we get to eat!" Joshua cried. He half ran, half galloped toward the tavern with Lily bouncing on his hip.

I was following close behind when I heard my name. "Remembrance? Remembrance Nye? Is that you?"

Someone here knew me? The voice was vaguely familiar, but I couldn't place it. I searched through the faces to find its owner. Then out from a knot of people came Alice Blodgett, my mother's best friend from Hartland. I ran to her, grateful to see a familiar face. She hugged me tight, then held me at arm's length to look at me. "I barely recognized you. You must be a foot taller than you were when I last saw you. How old are you now?"

"Thirteen," I said. I smoothed back my hair, aware that I must look a fright.

"I'm surprised to see you here. I thought you lived farther west." She looked around. "And where is the rest of your family?"

"That's my brother, Joshua, coming toward us, and the baby he's carrying is Lily, our little sister."

Mrs. Blodgett stepped back when she saw them. Lily's poor dress was grimy, and with all the bloody mosquito bites she looked as if she had been beaten. Joshua saw the look on Alice Blodgett's face and didn't come any closer. I could tell he didn't recognize her from home.

"A new baby? Why, I had no idea. It's been such a long time since I've heard from your mother. When people move away, it's so hard to keep in touch with them." Mrs. Blodgett's face showed concern now. She had known Mama well enough to realize she wouldn't allow her children to be in this condition unless something was terribly wrong. "Where is Aurelia, Mem?"

I didn't know how to tell her. I thought surely everyone at home must know about Mama by now. Was it possible that Grandma hadn't told them?

Mrs. Blodgett took my silence as her answer. "Oh, my dear, something has happened to her, hasn't it? Is she ill?"

"Mama fared poorly after the birth," I started out.

Mrs. Blodgett took my hands in hers. "Your mother didn't survive the birth?"

I was going to tell her how Mama went mad, but I stopped myself. "No," I said. "She didn't survive." In a way, that was the truth. The Mama I had known was gone after Lily arrived.

Mrs. Blodgett's eyes filled with tears, and she pressed her fist to her lips to keep from crying. "Oh, my poor Aurelia. I wish I had known. If only I had been close enough to help."

I thought of how different things might have been for Mama if she had given birth in Connecticut with friends like Alice Blodgett to comfort her. It took a few minutes before Mrs. Blodgett regained her composure. "How have you managed without her?" She wiped her eyes with a handkerchief. "You've raised the babe yourself?"

"Yes, Mrs. Blodgett, I've raised Lily."

"And your father? Is he well?"

Papa. How would I explain Papa and the fact that we were running away? I would simply tell the truth, that we were alone. Mrs. Blodgett might be willing to let us travel with them. Lily could ride in the wagon, and I could ride with her part of the time. "Papa is working on the Erie Canal, and I'm taking the children back to live with Grandma."

"You're traveling alone?"

"Yes, ma'am." I pulled out the handkerchief and started to untie the knot. "And I was wondering . . . I have some money. If I gave it to you to help pay for our food, could we travel with you?" I held out the coins in my palm. "I'd make sure Joshua and Lily weren't any trouble, and I could be of help to you along the way. I can cook and I . . ."

Mrs. Blodgett folded my fingers back over the coins. "Nothing would make me happier than to have you travel with us, Mem. But we're going in the wrong direction. We're heading west to Ohio."

"You've left Hartland?"

I tucked the coins back into my basket, ducking my head so she couldn't see the disappointment on my face.

"Are you sure your family is still in Hartland, Mem?"

I looked up, startled. "Of course. Why wouldn't they be there?"

"Perhaps you didn't hear about the terrible summer we had last year. There was snow in June and killing frosts all through July, August, and September. Many farmers failed to bring in crops."

"I know," I said. "We had the same thing in the Genesee Country."

"But probably not so bad as we had it in Hartland," Mrs. Blodgett insisted. "And the towns to the east of us were even harder hit. Many families have left Hartland. As a matter of fact, I think your aunt Lydia and her family sold their farm and left a week or so ago. They should be on the road ahead of us. I'm surprised you didn't run into them. And I know your aunt Sally's family is thinking of doing the same. They may have left already. Almost half of the people we know are either gone or leaving soon to get settled out west before the winter snows."

"But my grandmother must be there. She would have told us if they were moving." Then a terrible thought struck me. How would they tell us? Did anyone know we were living in Rome? Papa said he wrote to Grandma, but did he? And why didn't we hear from Aunt Lydia about their move? Were their letters going to the postmaster in Williamson, sitting unread?

Mrs. Blodgett bit her lip. "I don't know about your grandmother, Mem. Her health wasn't good last winter." She must have seen the look of panic in my eyes, because she added, "No, I didn't mean to imply that anything happened to her. It's just that I doubt she's up to such a long journey. But I really shouldn't be saying anything. Since Aurelia left, I've had little contact with your family."

"Alice! Time's a-wastin'."

Mrs. Blodgett turned at the sound of her name. "That's Caleb calling me. He's anxious to get started."

I nodded. The lump in my throat prevented me from speaking.

Mrs. Blodgett hugged me. "Oh, I hate to leave you like this. I only wish I knew you would be all right. Do you need money? I could ask Caleb . . ." Her voice trailed off.

"Oh, no. We have plenty," I managed to say. Mama wouldn't want me taking money from her best friend. It was bad enough that Alice Blodgett saw us looking so terrible.

"I didn't mean to upset you, telling you about Hartland, but you really should know what you're headed back to. If I run into your aunt Lydia on the road, I'll tell her I saw you."

"Alice!"

"I really have to go. Godspeed!" She turned and ran to the wagon where Mr. Blodgett waited impatiently.

I walked over to a bench in front of the tavern and sat down. My stomach pained me, probably from hunger. I watched the group of people milling around in front of the tavern. Two more wagons had just pulled in from the east. I realized that we hadn't seen any wagons filled with settlers heading back toward New England—only the stagecoaches with wealthy travelers like Mrs. Travis. It seemed to be just as Mrs. Blodgett had said. People were leaving New England in great numbers. But what did they hope to find out west? I watched the Blodgett wagon bounce along the road. Had Aunt Lydia bypassed Rome on the turnpike, not knowing that we were there? Was Aunt Sally already starting out on the journey west with her family?

And what of Grandma? Would they leave her and Grandpa all alone in Hartland? I pulled the locket out from my dress and held it tightly in my hand. "Oh, Grandma," I breathed. "Please be all right. Please be there when we get to Hartland."

"Who were you talking to?" Joshua said, plunking Lily beside me on the bench.

"Nobody," I said, ashamed to be caught talking to myself.

"I saw you. You were talking to some lady."

"Oh. That was Mrs. Blodgett from Hartland."

Joshua's face brightened. "Hartland? Can we ride with them?"

"No, they're leaving Hartland to move west."

Joshua kicked at a stone. "They'll be sorry."

Yes, they will, I thought. At least Alice Blodgett was likely to be sorry. I thought of her starting out for a new life just as Mama had done two long years ago. I had wanted to tell her that the great wilderness wasn't all it was cracked up to be, but I knew it wasn't my place to say anything. As in our family, it was probably the man who had made the decision to move. Still, I wished I had warned Alice Blodgett that the wilderness was wild and cruel and lonely enough to drive a gentlewoman from New England clean out of her mind. If somebody had said that to Mama, she'd still be alive and we'd all be in Connecticut where we belonged.

# Twelve

The meat at the tavern was expensive, so we could only afford some big crusty rolls and a shared glass of cider—a total of eight cents. I saved part of my roll in case we couldn't find food later. As we kept heading east, we met many wagons coming toward us. I searched each face, looking for Aunt Sally and her family, but the people were strangers.

It seemed that all of New England would be empty of people by the time we got there, although I'd heard that more ships than ever were carrying immigrants from Europe, hoping to find a new life in America. What did they think they were running to? Did they really expect their lives to be better heading west? If this kept up, there would be wagons streaming all across the Louisiana Purchase and out to the western coast of America. And what would they do when they got there?

Turn around and start the whole parade in the opposite direction? It made no sense to me.

The one good thing about our journey was that our days had a purpose. Now that Joshua was resigned to leaving Papa, he didn't fight me anymore. Other than getting cranky when he was tired, he was mostly amiable. Lily was more of a problem because she wasn't tired enough, so we had to spend part of the day slowed down to her pace while she insisted on walking. It was worth the time, though, because afterward she would allow herself to be carried, and we could make up lost time. Joshua was almost as strong as me now and could carry her for some distance without complaining.

As the late afternoon shadows stretched long, we approached a man squatted by a fire, cooking something on the bank of the river. Joshua started running ahead to see him, but I called him back. "You mustn't go up to strangers like that. You know what happened with the last one."

"I won't buy anything from him, Mem. I just want to see what he's doing." He turned and ran on.

Joshua was already sitting next to the man when I got there. "This is Jason, Mem. He's come up from Albany, and he's going to Rome to work on the canal with Papa." Joshua had been not more than two minutes ahead of me and he'd already learned this young man's story and probably told him all of our business as well.

Jason smiled. He was much younger than he'd seemed from a distance—not much more than Virgil's age, I suspected, but much better looking. "Joshua here says he's hungry. Can I offer you some beans?"

The emptiness in my stomach made me say yes, even though I was wary of him. He rinsed his tin plate in the river and dished up some for us to share, and we all ate our fill. I didn't say much, but Joshua prattled on about the canal and Papa. We finished our meal, and Jason poured water on the fire, then packed up, anxious to get on to Rome. "I'll tell your father I saw you. What's his name?"

I was going to make something up, but Joshua was too fast for me. "Jeremiah Nye."

What difference did it make? By the time Jason saw Papa, we'd be long gone. Probably past Albany.

We parted company and continued on our way. The scenery was beautiful here, the road running along the Mohawk River gorge. I picked a campsite for the night that was across the road from the river, back a short ways into the woods so we wouldn't be in plain sight of travelers. We had been cheated enough on our first two days of travel to make me wary of strangers. If people would cheat us out of our money, there was no telling what other harm they might do to us.

Sleeping that night was next to impossible. The roots from the trees made for a lumpy bed, and my stomach ached again. I tossed and thrashed, trying to get comfortable, but it was another battle with mosquitoes. Sometime in the middle of the night when the moon was high, I heard the screech of a mountain lion. That's when I wished I had spent the money to buy a tinderbox so we could have a fire. Here in the dark there could be all manner of wild creatures watching us, and we couldn't see them. I sat up for a while, straining my eyes to catch some movement in the dark. I listened to the cry of the mountain lion, trying to judge how far away it was. When I had first heard that sound on our journey to the wilderness, I had thought it to be a woman, screaming in fright. Knowing what it was now didn't make it any less scary.

Soon some wolves took up the cry. There seemed to be four of them, and I tried to keep from being frightened by trying to tell the voices apart. I hoped they weren't cries of hunger. Was it my imagination that they seemed to be drawing closer? When the moon lit a path through the trees, I looked around until I found a large club of a branch. I sat leaning against a tree and held my weapon as I watched over Lily's and Joshua's sleeping forms. Every crack of a twig made me jump.

❧ ❧ ❧

I awoke Thursday morning with the first light of dawn, grateful that the night was over but ashamed that I hadn't been able to guard my brother and sister through the night without falling asleep. How could I have slept when we might have been in such danger?

I stood and stretched, then went off to find a private place to relieve myself. It was there that I made the awful discovery. There was blood on my clothing. When I examined my legs, I found more blood, but no wound. Then I realized the bleeding was coming from somewhere inside me. Not long before we left Williamson, a young girl had started bleeding from her nose and mouth. Within two days she was in her grave. The doctor could do nothing to save her. And now the same thing was happening to me.

I sat down to think. My heart was beating so fast, I could feel it pounding in my throat. I didn't want to frighten Joshua by letting him know I was ill, but what if I wasn't strong enough to last the whole trip? Worse yet, what if I died in the middle of nowhere? Joshua wouldn't know what to do—where to go. I started to cry, and before I could stop, sobs were racking my whole body. What would become of Joshua and Lily? They'd lost a mother and a father and now their sister, too?

Well, it wasn't fair, but I couldn't just sit there blubbering about it. I needed to do something before it was too late. We had to start out right away for Grandma's house and just hope I could make it. But then I thought about Grandma. If she was already in poor health and if the rest of the family was moving away, was it fair to burden her with the care of two young children without me being there to help her?

That's when I realized the only person who could help was Papa. It no longer mattered if he wanted us or not. He'd just have to stop digging his stupid ditch and become a father again. I stormed back into our campsite and was about to wake Lily and Joshua when I thought of something. Though I knew I couldn't stop the bleeding, I didn't want to frighten Joshua and Lily by having the blood soak through my clothes. I took one of Lily's clouts behind the tree and fashioned it into a bandage that would catch the blood. Then I went back to wake them. "Lily, Joshua! Come! We're going back to Papa."

Joshua pulled up on his elbows. "What? What about Papa?"

"I said we're going back."

He sat up and scratched himself, still squinting through sleep. "Why?"

"Because it's too far to go to Grandma's and we don't have enough money to get us there." That was, after all, the truth.

Joshua was on his feet now. "But how will we get back to Papa?"

"The same way we got here," I said, gently shaking Lily to wake her. "We'll walk."

"But it's so far," Joshua whined.

"It's probably three times as far to Grandma's as it is

to Rome," I said. "Besides, you were the one who wanted to stay with Papa in the first place. You were right all along."

Joshua brightened. "I was?"

I gathered Lily in my arms. There wasn't time to wait until she was fully awake. "Yes, you were. Now let's get going."

As I picked up the basket, I noticed my journal. I wished I could stop to write in it, to tell Lily of my hopes for her and to let her know what her mother was like. Even Joshua's memory of Mama would fade without me being there to remind him of her. But there was no time for that now. The only comfort I could find in my situation was that I'd soon be reunited with Mama. And in heaven, Mama would be herself again—the Mama I used to know.

Joshua started off eagerly, gloating over his victory, and I followed, with Lily sleeping in my arms, her head rocking gently against my shoulder with each step.

Lily was awake by the time we stopped at the tavern for breakfast. When the serving girl came to our table, I began to order two bowls of mush. Then I changed my mind. "No, wait . . . two orders of eggs . . . with bacon."

Joshua's eyes widened. "Eggs and bacon? Did we get more money?"

"No. But since we're closer to Rome than to Grandma's, we won't need so many meals along the way." That was only part of it. If this was to be one of

my last meals, I wanted it to be a good one. I wasn't
going to eat another bowl of mush for as long as I lived.
That thought made me want to laugh and cry at the
same time.

We didn't take long to savor the meal. I knew it was
important to get started. I tried not to think about what
was happening to me as we walked along, though I
could tell that the bleeding continued. I was glad I had
thought of the bandage. Did I dare hope that my malady
wasn't fatal? Perhaps a doctor could help me, but I didn't
have much faith in that. From what I'd seen, once people
came down with unexplained illnesses, it wasn't long
before they were taken from this life.

I couldn't bear the thought of dying. Could this have
been my only purpose in life—to make Papa see that he
must take care of his family? No matter how hard I tried
to fill my mind with noble thoughts, it seemed a terrible
waste for me to go so soon. I tried silently bargaining
with God as we walked along, telling him all the things
I would do for others if he would only let me live. Just
think of all the children I could teach, I pleaded in my
mind.

Joshua brought me suddenly out of my thoughts.
"Are you mad at me?" he asked.

"No. What makes you ask that?"

"Your face is all scowly and scrunched up. Like this."
He pulled down his eyebrows and pursed his lips.

"Surely I don't look that bad."

"Yes, you do." He walked beside me, still making the face.

Though Joshua often vexed me, I couldn't help but smile at his antics. And I was thankful that he was so good with Lily. If the family did have to go on without me, he would be able to help Papa with her care.

Lily had fallen asleep again with her head on my shoulder. We were making good time as she slept, though my arms felt ready to pull out of their sockets.

I caught the sound of thunder in the distance. It wasn't long before a storm was upon us, slamming first wind, then a few drops of rain, then a wall of water hard into our faces. I pulled up my skirt in front to wrap around Lily, but it soaked through quickly and did little to protect her other than prevent the wind from taking her breath away. After pushing against the storm for only a short time, I could feel myself begin to weaken.

"Can't we stop and take shelter, Mem?" Joshua shouted. "If we stood behind that thick oak, we'd be protected from the wind."

I didn't dare stop for fear I wouldn't have the strength to continue. We had to make it back to Rome. "Keep going," I called back. "We have to keep going."

We hadn't seen any wagons since the storm began. Then suddenly there was one heading toward us, a small wagon with no top, with a lone horse and driver. "Joshua!" I shouted. "Get out of the way! Wagon coming!"

We stood at the side of the road waiting for it to pass, but the wagon stopped when it got to us. If the driver was offering us a ride, he should have seen that we were headed in the opposite direction. Then I realized it wasn't a man after all. It was Maude Tucker, huddled under a canvas tarp. "Don't just stand there gaping at me," she shouted over the wind. "Get yourselves into this wagon and cover up. Don't you have sense to come in out of the rain?"

I handed Lily up to her, then gave Joshua a boost and hauled myself into the seat beside him. I pulled the canvas around me, though it wasn't possible for me to get any wetter than I already was. Maude gave Lily back to Joshua and eased the horse around to go the other way.

"You came looking for us?" I asked when I finally managed to get over the shock of seeing her.

"Of course I came looking. You don't think I'm out in this downpour for my health, do you? It wasn't until yesterday I knew for sure you were gone. We've had so many new people in and out, I thought I might have missed you in the crowd."

"But how did you know . . ."

"Where to look? I started asking everybody who came in the tavern if they'd seen you. One young man who came in this morning said he'd shared a meal with you yesterday just west of Little Falls. I left right away. Thought I'd have to travel farther to catch up to you."

I was surprised Jason had reached Rome so quickly.

He must have walked all night. "I left a note in our room," I said. "You didn't find it?"

"I don't snoop through my customers' rooms." Maude stared straight ahead, deftly steering around the deepest ruts in the road. "Why did you turn around? Have a change of heart?"

I wanted to tell her about my illness, but not in front of Joshua. He'd find out soon enough. "Yes," I said. "A change of heart."

"Your pa will tan your hides when he hears you ran off."

"Are you going to tell him?"

She gave me a sharp look. "No, you are."

I nodded, making the raindrops drip off my nose. I was crying now, but it didn't matter. Maude would think it was only rain on my cheeks, if she cared.

"Mem says you don't like us," Joshua said, "but you wouldn't come after us if you didn't like us, would you?"

Maude's eyes were on the road. "Don't reckon I would."

Joshua poked me on the arm. "See?" he whispered. "She likes us."

"I—I never said that you didn't like us," I stammered. "I just thought we were a bit of a nuisance in the tavern."

"You had your hands full," Maude said.

I looked over at her. She sat hunched in the wagon seat, gripping the reins in her large chapped hands. She looked nothing like Mama. Nothing at all. And yet I felt safer here in the wagon with Maude than I had in a long time. She was gruff, but I knew that no matter what might befall us along the road, Maude would know how to handle it. I was still stunned that she had come after us. Perhaps I had misjudged her.

❧ ❧ ❧

Even at the slow pace of Maude's rickety old market wagon, the miles dropped away quickly. It wasn't long before we pulled into Utica. Maude passed by Bagg's Hotel and stopped in front of York House. "You hungry?"

"Yes!" Joshua said.

"He's always hungry," I said. "But I'm not. I could wait until we get back to Rome." I was anxious to return to Tucker's Tavern so that I could share my burden with her, but Joshua was already out of the wagon.

Maude laughed. "If you go back to my place, you'll be eating the meal that Virgil prepared. I expect I'll lose a few customers over that."

"Virgil is doing the cooking?" I asked.

"I had no one else to do it. That new serving girl couldn't boil water if you put it over the fire for her."

"Why do you keep Virgil on?" I asked. "He doesn't seem to work very hard."

Maude laughed. "That's the truth. I took him in three years ago when he'd just lost his whole family in a fire and had no other kinfolk to turn to. I just tried to keep him out of trouble is all. He's ready to go out on his own now."

So Maude took Virgil in just to be kind? I must have been staring, because Maude took my arm. "Come on. This is supposed to be the largest tavern west of New York City. I've heard tell of it from travelers. I might be givin' up the tavern business, but I've always had a hankerin' to see this one."

Maude carried Lily inside and brushed me away when I offered to take her. "It's been a long time since I've held a little one," she said. "Don't often get the chance."

Maude looked different to me. Then I realized it was the first time I'd seen her when her forehead hadn't been creased with the strain of trying to do six things at once. She set Lily on the table facing her and babbled nonsense words to her while she dabbed at the bloody mosquito bites with her handkerchief. Maude was almost pretty when she smiled. Well, maybe not pretty, but not altogether unpleasant, either.

Maude ordered stew for all of us. My stomach was too upset with worry for me to think of food, but it smelled good, and I ended up eating the whole bowl.

Maude kept up a running commentary about the food. "Too much pepper and garlic in the stew," she said. "When a cook does that, I get to wondering if the meat's gone bad and they're just trying to cover up the taste. That's an old restaurant trick, you know."

Luckily, or maybe unluckily, I had just licked the last traces of it from my spoon.

"For someone who wasn't hungry, you managed to make short work of that stew. Hope I was wrong about the rotten meat."

The rest of the trip home seemed to take forever. I couldn't tell if the rumbling in my stomach was from my illness or the stew, and I could still feel the bleeding. I only hoped my makeshift bandage would contain it a little longer. We rolled out of town, past a few small settlements and along the edge of the hills to Rome. All the time my mind was racing about what to tell Maude.

Finally we pulled up at the tavern. Virgil came out to meet us. "I see you found the runaways."

"They weren't running away when I found them," Maude said, handing him the reins. "They were coming back."

When we got inside, I sent Joshua up to the room with Lily and I followed Maude into the kitchen. "Lordy, will you look at the mess that boy made! It'll take me longer to clean up than it did for him to cook." She turned to me. "Did I hear you offer to help in exchange for the ride I just gave you?"

I tried to say something, but I burst into tears instead.

"Good heavens, girl, I'm not fond of washing dishes, either, but it *is* your job, you know. Course I suppose your running away tells me you quit. Is that it?"

"I have to tell you something," I gasped. "About why we came back."

She took a seat at the table and motioned me to sit across from her. "What is it, child?"

"I'm sick," I said. "And I had to bring the children back to Papa, because . . ." I had to take a deep breath before I could go on. "Because I think I may be dying."

Maude leaned forward and felt my forehead. "What makes you think that? You feel feverish?"

"No, it's nothing like that. It's something very strange." I could feel a sob welling up inside me. "I don't want to die! I don't want to be put into a box in the ground like Mama."

Maude moved quickly to my bench and put her arms around me. "There, there, child," she said, holding me close. "Whatever's wrong, we'll have it seen to. Don't you worry. You're going to be all right." She held me until I could stop the sobbing. "Tell me, now," she said softly. "What makes you think you're dying?"

My voice came out all thin and shaky. "I've had this pain for a while . . . in my stomach. And this morning I found blood. There's no wound. I'm just . . . I'm just bleeding from somewhere down inside."

Maude leaned back and looked at me. "How old are you, Mem?"

"Thirteen."

She hugged me again. "I can say with some confidence that you are not dying."

"I'm not?" How could she be so sure? She wasn't a doctor.

"No, you're perfectly healthy."

"I can't be. There was a girl in Williamson who began spitting up blood, and she died."

"That's different," Maude said. "Your bleeding is a natural thing. It'll happen to you for a few days every month until you're past your childbearing years."

I pulled away from her. "Why? What could be the purpose of that?"

"It's your lot as a woman," Maude said. "You'll get used to it."

"No, I won't!" I cried.

Maude laughed. "Oh, Lordy, you remind me so much of myself at your age. I thought God had done this just to annoy me. There's one thing that should be a comfort to you, though."

"What's that?" I asked.

"It's not as bad as dying, now, is it?"

I smiled through my tears. "No," I said. "Not quite."

Maude took me to her room and showed me how to manage my new condition. Then she went on and told me a powerful lot more than I ever wanted to know about how babies got started. "That's ridiculous," I said, only half believing what she had told me. "Now I'm *sure* I'll never get married."

Maude smiled. "That's what I said, but you just wait.

Someday a kind young man will come along and make you change your mind."

"I won't," I said. "I want to be a teacher, and teachers aren't allowed to marry."

"A teacher?" She nodded. "That's a fine profession. But if teaching is in your plans, you'd best get some more schooling."

"I will," I said. "As soon as we've settled back in . . . well, somewhere."

"I've been wantin' to ask," Maude said. "What made you run away, Mem?"

I was so glad to have someone take an interest, I told her everything. I blurted out the whole business about Papa not caring about us anymore and about how I'd tried to take us back to Grandma's. "Papa promised me he'd take us home," I said. "He promised me at Mama's funeral. But now he doesn't want to go."

Maude's eyes looked sad. "Sometimes people make promises they can't keep."

"I guess I found that out."

"We'll have this conversation another time," she said. "For now, let's just leave it be and see how things go when I talk with your papa Saturday night."

# Thirteen

I worried for the next two days about what Maude would say to Papa, but as I watched the way she handled the men who came into the tavern, I knew if anybody could deal with Papa and make things turn out all right, it would be Maude.

She got her chance Saturday night. We were about halfway through the meal when we heard a din outside and the canal workers stumbled into the room, already well into their Saturday night celebrating.

Papa didn't even notice us and was ready to sit down with his buddies when Maude called him over. He slid onto the bench next to her. "These children been giving you any trouble this week? Because if they have, I'll give them a talking to."

He gave us no greeting, just a quick smile.

Maude looked at me. "There was a problem."

Before she could say more, Papa called out to the serving girl who was carrying a tray of tankards. "I'll take one of those ales."

When the girl was almost to the table, Maude motioned her away. "No ale. You can drink yourself silly after we talk, but right now I need you to be sensible."

Papa's eyes narrowed, but he didn't object.

"These children tried to run away this week," she continued. "Back to Connecticut."

"Not me!" Joshua piped up—the little Judas. "It was all Mem's idea. I didn't even want to go. She made me go." I swung my foot under the table, trying to connect with his ankle, but he was sitting on his foot.

"That's right," Maude agreed. "Mem did some hard thinking about her situation and decided it was up to her to get the children back to where family would care for them."

Papa's face grew dark with anger. One thing he believed more than anything was that you didn't discuss family matters with strangers. That feeling was so strong in him, he had let Mama die rather than admit to anyone that she needed help. And now I had gone and talked to Maude. I looked down at my plate to avoid his glare.

"Perhaps Mem has forgotten that I promised to take

her back to Connecticut. In my own good time, I'll do just that."

"Oh, she hasn't forgotten that promise, Jeremiah. But it seems you're too late. Your wife's sisters are moving west. And the grandmother is probably too ill to take on the care of a young family."

Papa tore a hunk of bread from the crusty loaf in front of him. He stuffed it in his mouth and chewed for several long minutes, staring past me. "Well, that's the end of that, then. The children will just have to stay here the way they have been."

"That's not a good idea, Jeremiah. With the canal bringing in so many new people, Rome is changing. I don't think this will be a place you want to leave children unattended. Mem has a good head on her shoulders, but she needs someone to look after her and help her with the children."

"Well, the canal boss said we'll probably be moving the camp farther west before long, anyway. I'll have to find another place to put the children."

Another tavern? It could be even worse than it had been here. I looked to Maude for help, but she was concentrating all of her attention on Papa.

"You'll put these children somewhere else and do what with them? Work all week, carouse all Saturday night, sleep it off all Sunday, and go back to the camp for the next six days?"

Papa shrugged. "That's about how my week goes nowadays, so I can't be looking after my children, can I? Who am I going to get to watch over three children all week? If you're so worried about them, are you volunteering to be their mother?"

"Maybe I am," Maude said evenly, looking him straight in the eye. "Maybe I'm doing just that."

A slow grin crossed Papa's face, and he leaned toward Maude, nudging her with his shoulder. "Why, Maude Tucker, are you asking to be my wife? Because I'm thinking you'd be a fine mother for my children."

Maude shoved Papa away. "I've had a long parade of darn fools coming through here, but you're the poorest excuse for a man I've seen in quite some time. You're right about one thing, though. I would make a good mother for these children. I'd like to take them with me when I move on, if that's agreeable with you."

Papa looked surprised. "Move on?"

"I've been thinking of selling this place for a long time. I finally have a buyer with a good offer, and I'm going to take it."

"Where would you take them?" Papa asked. He didn't say he loved us and wouldn't let us go. He just asked where she would take us. He could have been inquiring about a team of oxen or some farm tools. We were nothing to Papa, and at that moment I knew Papa was nothing to me. Any small hope I had held of him coming to his senses and being a father again had disappeared.

But having Maude Tucker for a mother was another matter altogether. She'd been kind to us, but what right did she have to take us? "We don't need a new mother!" I cried. "I've been the mother to Lily and Joshua for over a year now, and we've managed just fine. I don't want a tavern keeper for a mother."

I regretted my words the second they left my lips. Maude looked as if I had slapped her. I hadn't meant to hurt her, but everything was happening too fast. I stood, almost tipping Joshua off the bench, and ran out of the room, out into the darkening street and through the town. I didn't stop until I came to the gatehouse to the fort. I ran inside and sat on the ground in the back corner, where I could hide in the shadows and not be seen from the street.

My life had changed so much in the past few days. First my only thought was to get to Grandma, then I had convinced myself I had only a short time to live. Now I had no idea what the future held. It had never occurred to me that Maude would want us. Why had she offered to take us in? Did she have a fondness for us, or did she just feel pity? Most likely she felt only anger now, after what I had said at the table.

Suddenly I heard voices coming nearer. I hoped it

wasn't the boys we had run into at the fort before. I tried to make myself as small as possible, shrinking into the shadows.

"I saw her come this way, Papa. I think she's over here." It was Joshua, giving away my hiding place. I stayed put, but Joshua led Papa right to me. "Here she is."

"So I see. Well, that was a pretty scene you made back at the tavern, Mem. What do you have to say for yourself?"

I didn't say anything, but inside I was screaming, "Me! What do *I* have to say for myself? I'm not the one who deserted my children. I'm the sensible one, remember?"

Papa took my silence for remorse. He slowly eased himself down next to me, and Joshua sat cross-legged, facing us. "It's all right, Mem. I know you're upset. Maybe it's a good thing we had this discussion today, because I'll be moving on soon."

"I know. You told us at dinner," I mumbled.

Papa rubbed his chin. It was a gesture he used when he was at a loss for words. "Well, it's more than just moving a ways down the canal. That's only the beginning."

"Where's Lily?" I interrupted. I wasn't interested in his plans.

Papa looked puzzled for a moment, as if he had forgotten about her. "Oh, she's fine. Maude has her."

She can't have her, I thought. Lily is mine.

"Mem, you have to understand what a grand project this is. When we had the farm, I was only trying to raise food to feed you children and your mother. But now I'm building a great waterway that will allow farmers in the Genesee Country to send their crops to people hundreds of miles away." He spread his arms like one of the pompous speakers we'd seen at the canal opening ceremony, and he talked as if he were digging the whole canal himself.

Even in the dimming light I could see the sparkle in his eyes, but I wasn't charmed by it anymore. This was the old Papa, all wrapped up in a new dream. His last dream took us all to the wilderness and killed my mother. His new dream had no room for us at all, and I was thankful for that. "Do you understand what I'm saying, Mem?"

"Well, certainly I can see how building the great Erie Canal would be much more important to you," I spat out the venom-filled words. "Why content yourself with farming for your own little family when you can save the whole world?"

Papa reached over and gave me a one-armed hug. He smelled of whiskey. "Don't you see my point, Mem? I'm going to follow the building of the canal all the way to Buffalo. Can you imagine the celebration when we finally finish it? It's the most valuable work I've ever

done, and I want to be on that first boat that travels all
the way back to Albany."

Joshua looked up at Papa with such hope in his eyes,
I wanted to slap him until he had some sense. "But
we'll be with you, won't we, Papa? You'll take us along
while you build your canal? And we can take that boat
ride with you?" I heard the little click in his throat that
meant Joshua was near tears, even though he was
smiling.

Papa patted him on the head. "We won't always be
near a town like this, son. It won't be long before we're
digging through the great Montezuma Swamp." He made
another grand sweep of his arms. "That's no place for a
man to take his family."

"But where will we be?" Joshua's tears spilled over
now.

Papa made some aimless gestures, as if he hoped his
hands would give him the words he needed, but he
ended with a shrug. "I think Mrs. Tucker made a most
generous offer. . . ."

I felt a rage building inside me. I didn't care about
his stupid canal. All I wanted was a father, but that job
wasn't important enough for Papa anymore.

"But Papa," Joshua persisted. "When will we ever see
you again?"

I stood up. "Joshua? Papa doesn't want us anymore.
He's giving us away. Isn't that right, Papa?"

Papa had no answer to my question. I pulled Joshua to his feet and started dragging him back to the tavern. Papa didn't try to come after us, and I was glad. If Maude Tucker still wanted us, then she'd get us.

It was better than nothing.

# Fourteen

We found Maude in the kitchen. She had washed Lily, so you could barely see her mosquito bites, and she'd put her in a clean new dress.

"What did you do with Lily's dress?" I demanded.

Maude glanced over her shoulder at me. "If I had any sense, I would have burned it, but I thought you might take offense. I can see I was right."

"Well, nobody asked you to buy her a new dress."

Maude handed Lily to me. "It's not new. It belonged to my daughter."

"I didn't know you had a daughter."

"She died when she was six. Scarlet fever."

I hadn't expected that. "Oh," I mumbled, shifting Lily to my hip. "I'm sorry." I couldn't be surly with someone who'd just told me about the death of her child. I wondered what more there was about Maude Tucker that I didn't know.

Joshua had slid onto the bench beside Maude. She saw his tear-stained face and pulled him close to her, brushing the hair out of his eyes. He leaned into her shoulder and sobbed. She rested her cheek on his head and rocked him, much as she had with me the night I thought I was dying. Poor Joshua. He needed a mother and a father, and all he had was a cranky older sister who spent the better part of each day scolding him for things that weren't entirely his fault.

When Joshua's breath stopped coming out in hiccups, Maude went to the cupboard and brought out two cookies. "Here, now, Joshua. You take Lily on up to your room and have these treats. Mem will be up to keep you company as soon as she and I have a talk."

He took the cookies and slid off the bench, coming over to collect Lily from me. I was about to admonish him for not thanking Maude for the cookies but thought better of it.

As I took a seat across the table from Maude, a sticky silence settled over the room. She started folding napkins, waiting, I knew, for my apology. I finally managed the courage to speak. "I'm sorry I was nasty to you before. It was a terrible thing to say. I didn't mean it."

Maude shrugged, still concentrating on the napkins.

"It was more my fault than yours. I would have told you what was on my mind, but it didn't really come to me until I saw what a darn fool you have for a father." I could tell from the look on her face and the way the corner of her mouth twitched that she was trying to figure a way to say something else. Finally she looked up. "What do you think about you children coming along with me?"

"Where would we go?"

"With the money I'm getting from the tavern, we'll be able to go anywhere we want. But you need to know something. I've been fixing to find out why all these wagons are heading west. I want to see what's out there."

"I can tell you what's out there," I said. "There's nothing but trees. The loneliness drove my mother mad."

Maude reached over and touched my arm. "The wilderness is hard on some women, Mem. I'm truly sorry about your mother, but I'm not trying to drag you back through all that hurt. I have no interest in carving a homestead out of virgin forest. There are cities out there, like Buffalo and Zanesville . . . and who knows what's beyond."

Was Maude just like Papa—off to chase a dream? Had we only traded one bad situation for another? But what choice did we have? Short of moving into the poorhouse, Maude was our only hope.

She must have read the thoughts on my face. "You don't seem none too pleased with the prospect of moving west. Am I right?"

I sighed. "It's not what I had in mind, but maybe I'll get used to the idea." What else could I say to her? What else could I do? Maybe if I were alone, I could strike out on my own and find a place for myself back in Connecticut. But I had Joshua and Lily to care for. When I really thought about it, I'd be hard-pressed to take care of myself, much less provide for them.

"Well, you'll have some time to mull it over," Maude said, "because I'm thinking our first stop should be to visit your grandmother in Connecticut."

I was too stunned to speak.

Maude pretended to fuss with the napkins again, waiting for my response. Finally she looked up. "Look, Mem. I'll take care of you children for as long as you want. That's a promise, and you can depend on me not to break it, long as I can still take a breath. But when we get to your grandma's . . . well, if you decide to stay with her, you're not going to hurt my feelings none, hear? I can head out west perfectly fine by myself. That's what I'd planned to do in the first place."

"You would do that? You'd take us all the way back to Connecticut? That would be so far out of your way."

Maude nodded. "I know, but if that's where you need to go, that's where I'll take you."

❧    ❧    ❧

The next day, when Virgil found out Maude was selling the tavern and leaving, he signed up to work full-time on the canal. He packed up the things in his room and came to Maude for his wages, not even thanking her for the three years she had given him room and board and extra money in exchange for the little work he managed to do around the tavern.

"I don't know what there is about this canal," Maude said that night. She was helping me with the dishes because Temperance had the night off. "It sure does have a pull on the menfolk."

"It's the money and the whiskey," I said, drying a tankard. "Least that's what got to Papa."

"You're prob'ly right. It's a powerful combination." Maude sighed. "I'd like to think my husband wouldn't have fallen victim to it."

"Your husband?" I hadn't heard her mention him before, though I'd wondered about him.

Maude plunged her hands into the soapy basin. "He was killed in the war. He was a good man. The day he left, I knew I'd never see him again, even though he promised to come back. Just had a cold feeling in my heart."

"I'm sorry," I said.

When Maude looked up, I saw tears in her eyes. "I thought I could keep things going with the tavern until he came back. I never intended to run it alone for good. The heart sort of went out of me when he was killed. That's why I was so glad to get a good offer on this place."

"But why are you helping us?" I asked. "I don't understand why you want to take on three children when you don't have to. We're not even related to you."

"I have my reasons. One is my daughter, Betsy. If she had lived, she'd be almost your age by now. I had two other babies after her, but they were sickly. Neither one lived to the first birthday." She shook her head. "I always wanted a family more than anything, but all my babies are in the cemetery."

It gave me a chill at first to think we would be taking the place of Maude's dead children. But now I understood why she wanted us, and it wasn't such a bad reason.

Maude sat down sideways on the bench, leaning one elbow on the table. "Here's another thing. I get a chance to make good money selling this tavern and smack at the same time you come along, needing some help. The way I look at it, those two things are connected. Sometimes you just know the right thing to do."

❦    ❦    ❦

The preparations for leaving took all week. Maude sold the wagon and bought a carriage with a top over it in case of rain and a small trunk for our things. She didn't take much of anything from the tavern. "That's from before," she said. "What we need from now on, we'll get new."

Thursday morning Maude sat Joshua on a tall stool and gave him a haircut that left a white band around his neck and face where the skin hadn't seen sunshine for a long time. It reminded me of the way he and Papa had looked when Mama gave them haircuts before the cabin raising at our homestead.

"You're a handsome lad," Maude told him. "You're grandma will be proud of you."

"I don't remember my grandma," he said, scratching at his neck where the bits of itchy hair had fallen.

"Oh, you have a memory of her somewhere inside. You'll know her when you see her again."

Joshua nodded. "I think she'll like me."

Maude smiled and brushed the hair from his shoulders. "I expect she will. Now why don't you go show off your new haircut." She gave him a little pat on the backside as he climbed off the stool and ran out of the room.

I stayed in the kitchen and swept up Joshua's hair. I noticed it was no longer blond but turning darker with more red in it, like mine. Mama had called it maple-syrup colored. As I pulled the broom over the wood planks I got thinking about Grandma and how Joshua didn't remember her at all. I could still see her in my mind, but I wondered what she would be like now. Would she be too ill to know us anymore? Lost deep in my thoughts, I managed to back into Maude, almost upsetting a tray of plates she was moving to the table.

"Whoa, girl! Keep your mind on what you're doing here. I don't want to buy a new set of dishes for the next owner."

"Sorry. I was just thinking."

Maude set the tray on the table. "I can see that."

"Hearing you and Joshua talk about Grandma got me wondering about something. I'm not sure we should go back to Connecticut."

Maude looked up, eyebrows raised. "Oh? Why not?"

"Well, we would only be going back to say good-bye, and Grandma and I did that when we left two years ago. I don't think she ever expected to see us again."

"That's possible," Maude said. "Most older folks never see their loved ones after they move away."

"And I was thinking . . . this is a new start for Joshua, Lily, and me. It seems to me we shouldn't begin by heading in the opposite direction of where we want to go."

A smile began to spread across Maude's face. "So you mean you're choosin' to go with me? Right from the start?"

I smiled back. "Yes. That's exactly what I mean. I'll write to Grandma so she knows we're heading west."

"There's going to be a real need for schoolteachers out there. We'll have to make sure you get the schooling you need."

"I'd like that," I said.

Maude came around the table and gave me a hug. "This is a new start for all of us, Mem. I have a feeling things will be a lot better from now on."

❧    ❧    ❧

On Friday, Maude bought clothes for all of us. Not fancy clothes, but good, serviceable ones. She bought herself a dress that buttoned all the way up to the neck, and she looked downright respectable in it. The only frivolous things she got were a small hat with green feathers for herself and one with little blue velvet ribbons for me.

Later that night I went through our things to pack them up. As I was cleaning out the dresser drawer, I found the tiny Herkimer diamond. I held it up to the candle and watched it change colors in the light of the flickering flame. It hadn't brought us the luck I'd wanted, but it might have given us something better. Only time would tell. I opened the locket and slipped it in among the curls of hair. I wasn't really superstitious, but I couldn't see any sense in leaving a good luck charm behind. That was only tempting fate.

I sat on my bed and opened my journal—all those empty pages waiting to be filled. Would I someday write about my students in this book? I ran my thumb along the edges of the pages, flipping them open one by one. If only I could read the words that would fill them, I'd know what my future would be. I knew one thing for certain. From now on I would write every day, and when my journal was full, I'd get another. I wanted to put it all down, everything that happened, so I could look back someday and see where I'd been, what I'd done. I thought about writing down how I felt, but my head was too full to find words. Instead I leaned back on my pillow.

❧ ❧ ❧

Saturday morning everything was in readiness for our journey, and Maude completed the sale of the tavern. She helped me twist and pin my hair up high in the back and placed my hat so it tilted forward at a jaunty angle. "Now you look like a real lady," she said as we studied ourselves in the mirror. "We clean up right good, don't we?" We laughed at our reflections, and I had to admit we looked just fine.

Maude sat straight and proper in the carriage seat as we drove through town, nodding to some of the people she knew. It wasn't until we were on the open road that she threw back her head and let out a whoop,

"Whoohee!" loud enough to near scare the horse to death. Then we all laughed. Joshua got so silly over it, I thought he'd fall from the carriage.

So we started off for Utica, since that was where we would find the turnpike to carry us out west. I had the same excited feeling as when I had walked next to Papa as we left Connecticut. I could still hear his words. "Put this day in your memory, daughter," he had said. "You're taking the first steps to a new life."

And now another new beginning. How many new lives could a person have—nine, like a cat? I couldn't help but think how badly the last venture had turned out, and I shivered. Maude reached over and squeezed my hand. "You scared?" she asked.

"A little," I said.

"Me too." She snapped the reins to pick up our pace. "But I'm not going to let that stop us."

We didn't meet any wagons for the first few miles. Then we saw a figure coming toward us in the distance, wearing the familiar slouch hat of a canal worker. He raised his hand to flag us down.

"What's a canal worker doing on the road this time of day?" I asked. "And aren't they digging closer to town?"

"They're clearing brush and trees out this way," Maude said. "Virgil told me that's the crew your pa is on now."

I felt my throat tighten at the mention of Papa. "I

hope we don't see him," I said. "I don't care if I ever talk
to him again."

Maude slowed the horses. "Unless I run him down, I
don't see a way to get around that."

I didn't understand her meaning until we were close
enough to make out the face of the man in the road.
"It's Papa! Why isn't he working?" For a fleeting moment
I hoped he had quit his job and was coming to get us.
But knowing Papa, I doubted that.

Maude reined the horses to a full halt.

"Papa?" Joshua jumped from the wagon and ran to
him.

"This will only get Joshua all stirred up again," I whispered to Maude. "Why couldn't he just leave things the
way they were?"

"Let him say what's on his mind," Maude said. "It
doesn't have to change anything. Just hear him out."

"There's nothing more to talk about," I insisted. "I'm
not getting out of the wagon."

"Then I will." Maude secured the reins, slipped to the
ground, and reached up to take Lily from me.

Out of the corner of my eye I saw Papa sitting on
a fallen log at the edge of the road with Joshua. Joshua's
arms were wrapped around Papa's middle, and he was
sobbing into his shirt. Papa clearly hadn't come to
reclaim us. It surprised me to realize I had been keeping
that hope in some corner of my heart.

I sat stiff in the wagon seat, staring at my hands which were clasped together so hard the knuckles had turned white. I wanted to shout for Maude to gather the children back to the wagon so we could leave and be done with this, but I held my tongue, because another part of me wanted to run to Papa—wanted to make one last plea to keep the family together. There was no sense trying to fight my tears. They flowed freely from the battle waging inside me.

I felt the wagon lurch and looked up to find Papa in the seat next to me. Maude had both Lily and Joshua now. I could see that Joshua was completely undone. Seeing Papa again was like pulling the scab off a wound that had barely begun to heal. "Mem, I just want you to know that I'm sorry."

What did he expect me to say? It's all right, Papa? Because it wasn't. And sorry for what? Because he gave us away to a stranger?

Papa reached over and touched my chin, turning my face toward him. "Do you know how much you take after your mama? Every time I look at you, I see her and it breaks my heart. There isn't a day goes by that I don't think of her."

I couldn't speak, but the voice inside my head was pleading. *Think of me, Papa. Think of Lily and Joshua. Mama's gone, but we're still here.*

But the other voice in my head simply said, *Tell us good-bye, Papa. Let us go and be done with it.*

I pulled away from Papa's hand so I wouldn't have to look at him. Maude was walking Joshua and Lily farther on down the road. I knew she was trying to give me my last chance to talk to my father, but words wouldn't come to me.

"I don't blame you for being angry, Mem. I've made a mess of things, right from the first moment we left Connecticut. Your mother would still be alive if it weren't for me. I've wrecked our whole family."

I looked up at him, surprised to see tears in his eyes. We sat in silence for several long minutes until Papa spoke.

"I have good news, Mem. I've been promoted to axman—a whole dollar's wages every day."

The canal again. I didn't want to hear about his rotten stinking canal. "What will you do when the canal is finished?" I asked. "It can't last forever, you know."

Papa's face brightened. "Don't you see? That's when I'll send for you children. By then I'll have money saved up. Maybe I'll start my own business. I've always thought I'd make a good merchant. I'll have a store right on the canal so I can carry goods shipped in from faraway places."

I stopped listening to Papa as he rambled on about his plans. He would always be chasing dreams, taking up a new scheme when the old one failed. But I knew dreams wouldn't put food on the table and a roof over our heads.

Papa reached over and took my hand. "If I thought I could be a decent father to you children right now, I'd do it. Fact is, I can't, Mem, and I'm not proud of that. But someday we'll live in a fine house and I'll be able to give you children all the things you deserve."

I nodded and pulled my hand away. Papa leaned over and kissed me on the cheek, then swung down from the wagon. Tears blurred my sight for a few minutes, and when I finally looked up, there was no sign of him—only Maude bringing Lily and Joshua back to the wagon.

"You ready to move on?" she asked, handing Lily up to me.

"Yes. Let's get as far away from here as we can."

Joshua squeezed onto the seat next to me and burrowed his head into my shoulder. I freed up one arm from Lily and put it around him. "Don't worry," I said. "We're going to be fine."

We rode along in silence for miles. Maude knew when you needed to be quiet. I was glad that Papa had come to say good-bye, even though it upset Joshua to see him. Papa hadn't meant to hurt us. He wasn't a bad man, but he was weak. Without Mama, he was completely lost. There was no way that Joshua, Lily, and I could take her place for him.

But somehow it seemed that Maude might be able to take the place of both Mama and Papa for us. I looked at her holding the reins in those big rough hands and remembered the day she came after us. Was that only a little over a week ago? And was it only a few days earlier that I had hated her so?

I surely hadn't planned on liking Maude Tucker, but I knew I was a whole lot more like her than I ever would be like Mama. Mama had been beautiful and fragile, like an apple blossom whose petals could be blown away in a breeze. Maude was an oak, solid enough to come through a tornado without losing a twig.

I fingered the gold locket that had been handed down in our family for over a hundred years and remembered the day that Grandma had given it to me. She had said I should wear it close to my heart to remind me of my connections to my family. She told me family was the most important thing in life.

Maude brought me out of my thoughts. "What are you smiling about, Mem?"

"Nothing," I said.

But I was thinking that someday I might want to give that locket to Maude. Maybe we didn't come from the same blood, but Maude had saved us when nobody else cared. If that wasn't being family, I didn't know what was.

As I looked down the road ahead, I knew it didn't matter how far we traveled or where we put down roots. I was already home.

# Author's Note

I had thought early on that this book might have some connection to the Erie Canal, since it fell into the right time period and Mem and her family could pass near the site of the canal opening ceremonies on their trip back to Connecticut. A great deal of information is available about the canal in its heyday and about the construction through the Montezuma Swamp and the succession of locks at Lockport. Except for detailed accounts of the opening ceremonies, it was more difficult to find information about the beginnings of the canal. At the Rome Historical Society in Rome, New York, I came across Daniel E. Wager's *Rome, New York—Our City and Its People*. The detailed descriptions of the buildings in Rome from its very beginnings helped me piece together what Mem might have seen walking around town in the summer of 1817.

I like to be able to visualize the place I am writing about, so I was delighted to learn that Fort Stanwix had been restored to its Revolutionary War condition. By 1817 the fort had fallen into disrepair, but seeing it in its original form helped me picture what it would have looked like when Joshua "discovered" it. As I approached the restored fort I was amazed to find that it was barely visible above the landscape, the ten- or twelve-foot pickets in the trench looking like little more than a garden fence.

The detailed 1817 maps in *Stafford's 1824 Guide for New York Travellers* listed the exact distance between landmarks, so I could estimate how long it would take for the stagecoach trip to Utica and Mem's walk eastward.

I love to find facts that readers will enjoy, such as the story of the canal workers going into the swamp naked from the waist down. This gave me a situation that would make Mem even more upset about her father working on the canal.

Prices in 1817 were important to the plot. I had to know how much Mem would have by keeping one week's room and board money and how far it would go toward getting her back to Connecticut. At the Ontario Historical Society in Canandaigua, New York, where I had done research for the earlier books—*Journey to Nowhere* and *Frozen Summer*—I had hoped to find newspaper ads to give me prices for the things Mem

might buy on her trip. It was exciting to read a copy of
the *Ontario Repository* from the actual week Mem
would have been traveling, but though there were many
ads, the prices were never mentioned. The historical
society staff pointed out that during that time, people
often bartered. Storekeepers' ledgers from 1817 showed
that customers brought in produce to sell and bought
goods. Whether or not actual money changed hands, it
gave me the price references I needed. Even though the
young country of America had its own currency at this
point in our history, English currency was still in wide
use. For the ease of comparing prices in Mem's time
with those of today, I opted to use the American currency, with the exception of the shillings given to Mem
by the English traveler, Mrs. Travis.

I did find a treasure tucked in a folder at the Ontario
Historical Society. It was a small card, an 1817 menu
from the elegant Blossom's Hotel in Canandaigua. I
thought readers would like to know that people really
ate the "fried calves' head with brain sauce" listed as a
side dish, so I used it in the hotel scene in Utica.

I pored over stagecoach schedules from 1817 and
was delighted to find that the coach Mem would have
taken from Utica left at three in the morning. I had orig-
inally written the scene as taking place after breakfast
but found it much more poignant to have it play out in
the middle of the night. I was surprised to learn how

expensive stagecoach travel was. It seemed odd that a person could get a full dinner at a tavern for twelve cents but would have to pay the same amount for just a one-mile journey in a stagecoach.

Shortly after the period covered in this book, life in New York State changed dramatically. Up until 1817 only a trickle of settlers had moved into western New York, making their way over rough turnpikes, partial river routes, and portage paths. The opening of the Erie Canal created cities almost overnight as great numbers of people were given easier access to the new land. Though the packet boats were crowded and passengers had to be prepared to duck when they came to a low bridge, it was far more comfortable than the bone-crunching rides over the rutted turnpikes and corduroy roads.

Building the canal was a long process and filled with hazards. Many workers died during construction through the Montezuma Swamp, falling victim to malaria. Even by wearing a Montezuma's necklace, a pot of smoldering wet leaves and sticks around his neck, a worker couldn't fully protect himself from the mosquitoes that carried the disease. At Lockport, where the canal would have to rise seventy feet, blasting through the solid rock of the Niagara escarpment, a huge colony of rattlesnakes made the work even more dangerous.

It wasn't until the fall of 1825 that the canal was completed and Governor Clinton led a first procession of boats from Buffalo to New York City. Welcoming celebrations were held in canal towns all along the way. The one exception was the city of Rome, whose people were upset that the canal had passed half a mile south of the city instead of flowing through it. They marched to the canal to the sound of muffled drums and poured a black barrel full of tar into the water as the parade of boats approached.

If Mem had waited for the canal to be finished before Papa came to her aid, she would have been twenty-one, looking after fourteen-year-old Joshua and nine-year-old Lily. It seems odd to me that I'll no longer be following Mem as she sets forth from this point. I thoroughly enjoyed watching her learn and grow through these three books. Ending this trilogy feels much the same as when we took our daughter off to college—a sense of something ending for me but beginning for her. I'll miss Mem, but it's time for her to go off on her own. I wish her well.